Jed Harker Rides Out

Jed Harker wishes for nothing more than to mind his own business while travelling north to Kansas. In the summer of 1861, men and women were taking sides all across the United States and Harker finds himself compelled to declare where he stands on slavery. The result is that he finds himself fleeing through the Indian Nations, helping a family of escaping slaves to freedom. With war about to break out, it will be a race against time for Harker and his wards as they become embroiled in the opening shots of the War Between the States.

Jed Harker Rides Out

Simon Webb

A Black Horse Western

ROBERT HALE

© Simon Webb 2018
First published in Great Britain 2018

ISBN 978-0-7198-2838-6

The Crowood Press
The Stable Block
Crowood Lane
Ramsbury
Marlborough
Wiltshire SN8 2HR

www.bhwesterns.com

Robert Hale is an imprint
of The Crowood Press

The right of Simon Webb to be identified as
author of this work has been asserted by him
in accordance with the Copyright, Designs and
Patents Act 1988

CHAPTER 1

It was a bright, clear morning in the early spring of 1861 and Jed Harker, having shaken the dust of Arkansas from his feet, was riding north to Missouri. Things had not worked out as well for Harker as he might have hoped and he had determined to make a fresh start of it in the north. Everywhere he looked, there were signs of a growing siege mentality on the part of those living in the southern states and this went hand in hand with a mistrust and dislike of Yankees such as himself. It was this, as much as anything else which had impelled him to head north. Although very far from being an ardent abolitionist, Harker had seen enough of the institution of slavery over the last few years to convince him that it was not to his taste. The longer he lingered in the south, the more distasteful he found the manifestations of the system; men and women being treated as chattels and goods, rather than as fellow beings. Harker

5

thought how glad he would be to leave such a sorry and unnatural state of affairs behind him.

So bound up was Harker in his own thoughts, as he trotted the mare along a rocky defile which gradually opened out into a broad plain, that he did not take as much heed of his immediate surroundings as was usually the case. Had he been paying just a little more attention to the road ahead and the view on either side, then he would perhaps have noticed that somebody was about to fire on him. As it was, he had just caught sight of a wagon or cart standing by the side of the track, about a hundred yards ahead of him, when there came the crack of a rifle and a musket ball passed so close to his head that he heard it droning by like a hornet. He reined in and made no move which could be interpreted as being hostile. It was as plain as a pikestaff that somebody had the drop on him and all that he could do was bide his time and see what chanced next. What he could not, in his wildest imaginings, have expected to happen was what actually did next occur; a woman's voice called out, confident and sharp, 'Throw down any weapon you're a carrying of, or 'fore God I'll kill you at once!'

'I only got my pistol,' Harker shouted back. 'I set a store by it and I'd as soon as not dash it to the ground.' As he bellowed these words, he peered over to where he supposed the woman was hiding, which was a stand of pines, surrounded by scrubby bushes. It was perhaps forty or fifty yards away. He couldn't see anybody, but knew that whoever was hidden there could surely see him. That shot had been a mite too close for comfort.

'You love that gun o' your'n more'n your life, then just you carry on down that road and see where it gets you,' came the reply. 'Drop it or you're dead.'

Jed Harker was possessed of a powerful instinct for self-preservation which had served him well during the thirty-two years of his life and he sensed that if he didn't cooperate, then there would be no further parlaying. He would end up with an ounce of lead through his brains. Very slowly and carefully, he lifted the Navy Colt from where it was tucked casually into his belt and dropped it in the dirt.

Harker had no idea what sort of woman might have been drawing down on him. He supposed that it might be some rough-looking cracker or the wife of a mountain-man. The person who emerged from the undergrowth though looked more like a school teacher. She walked towards him, with a rifle held at high port; ready for instant action. When she was close enough to speak without raising her voice, the woman, who was perhaps five years younger than Harker himself, said, 'Your friends are dead and 'less you do as you're bid, you're apt to fetch up the same way. You follow my meaning?'

'Well now, I don't rightly understand you,' said Harker, 'I've no friends hereabouts as I know of. Happen you've mistook me for another?'

There was silence, as the woman weighed Harker's

words. She was a hard one to read and it would not much have surprised him if this stranger had suddenly raised her gun and shot him down like a dog. She did nothing of the sort but said instead, 'Not a half hour since, five men rode down on us and there was shooting. Two of them was killed and so too was my friend, who lies over by yon wagon. Do you take oath and swear you had no part of this?'

'Ma'am, I left Gordon's Landing not three hours since. I was helping run the livery stable there 'til the back end of last week. Why I'd want to bushwhack you out here is somewhat of a mystery to me.'

'You're a Yankee?'

'Then what? Yes, I'm from New York.'

'I guess that lets you out of the cart then, for those as ambushed us was southrons through and through.'

The woman bent down and picked up Harker's pistol. Still holding her own weapon one-handed – but in a capable way, as though she could bring it up and fire quick enough should need arise – she reached up to where Harker sat astride his horse, offering him the pistol hilts first. She said, 'You can go. Sorry for firing on you. I was spooked.'

Harker smiled slightly and said, 'Judging from your shooting, I wouldn't have said you was spooked none. I'll warrant you could've taken me down in a second, had you been minded to do so.'

'That's nothing to the purpose. The day's wearing on and I've work to do, even if you've not.'

'You got grit and that's a fact,' said Harker admiringly. 'Still and all, maybe I can help. Not that I don't reckon as you can proceed well enough under your own steam. You're bound for Missouri?'

The young woman said nothing for a few seconds and Harker had the impression that two opposing impulses were contending for mastery in her breast. At length, she said, 'Truth is, I got a difficulty. You know aught of wagonry?'

'Like I said, I was helping run the livery stable over in Gordon's Landing. I reckon I know more than the next man about wagons and stages. Why?'

'In the flight from those villains as was chasing us, there's some mischief been wrought to my wagon. Like as not, it's a simple enough matter to remedy, but I'm blessed if I know what wants doing to it.'

'You want I should take a look?'

She shrugged. Jed Harker chuckled and said, 'You're a rare charmer and no mistake. You answer to any name or is that a secret?'

'Tyler. Abigail Tyler.'

'Which d'ye prefer as I should call you, Abigail or Miss Tyler?'

'I don't give a damn what you call me. You think you're at a barn dance or some such, sweet-talking some silly little girl? If you can aid me with that wagon, I'll be obliged. Otherwise, you can take yourself off.'

Shocked to hear such language from a woman, Harker suffered the mare to walk on in the direction of the wagon. The woman walking at his side said nothing more and seeing as she'd made it pretty plain that she'd no use for idle chatter, he too remained silent.

When they came nigh to the wagon, Harker dismounted and went over to see what the problem might be. He saw at once that there were two corpses lying nearby. He said to Abigail Tyler, 'Afore I mix myself up in this affair, you mind telling me who these men are and how they died?'

For a moment, she looked as though she was on the verge of telling him to go to the devil, but it was obvious that she needed his assistance if she were to be able to continue her journey. She said briefly, 'This man is, was, my business partner. T'other's one o' them as attacked us. There was another killed, but his horse rode off with him. I shot him; my partner, he shot this man here, before another of 'em got him.'

Harker went over to the wagon and looked to see what it might contain. All he could see were two stout crates and a couple of carpet bags. The canvas hood was folded up and stowed next to the other gear, turning what looked like a regular prairie schooner into an ordinary cart. He said, 'What were they after? You got something valuable here?'

'I reckon that's my business,' said the other shortly. 'Can you help me get this moving or are you just going to stand there asking a lot of damn-fool questions?'

'Your language is something else again, you know that?'

When there was no answer, he looked under the wagon and saw at once what was amiss. The brake beam had jerked loose, probably from banging over a rock, and was jammed tight against the rear wheels. Abigail Tyler said, 'Well, can you mend it?'

Harker straightened up and said, 'If you've a hammer, I can. We'll have to unload the whole wagon first.'

'Unload it? Why?'

By now, he'd had just about enough of this sharpness and said, 'Because if you want my aid, then that's what I'll have done. I don't aim to push a loaded cart round. We'll have to unhitch your oxen as well.'

The woman looked around uneasily and said, 'You know how long this is likely to take? Those as tried to rob us might return.'

'How many were there?'

'There were five, but two are dead.'

'Which makes three of them to us two, always assuming I consent to lend a hand. But why would they try again? What have you got here that's worth so much to'em?'

'You want to lend me a hand unhitching the oxen?' said Abigail. 'Then we can unload the cargo.'

Together, the two of them undid the harness and then hobbled the oxen so that they could graze on the sparse, scrubby grass. Then Harker jumped up into the wagon, with a view to shifting the crates

11

down. He found at once that they were too heavy for him to manage by himself. He said, 'Lord a mercy, what've you got in these here boxes? Lead?' Then a sudden thought came to him and he said, 'Tell me it's not gold? It surely weighs enough!'

'Gold, nothing! It's machine parts, if you must know. Push the crate over to the back and we can heave it down together.'

Between the two of them, they succeeded in getting the crates unloaded from the wagon and fortunately, there was a hammer among the tools stored in the chest under the driver's seat. It took Harker only fifteen minutes or so to loosen the brake-bar and so free the wheels. Just as he finished, Abigail Tyler came over and said, 'Don't like to alarm you, but we got company.' She gestured to the open country, where three riders could be seen advancing down the road in their direction.

'Would those be the same boys that you already had a run-in with?' asked Harker.

'Couldn't swear to it, but I reckon so.'

'Is there but the one rifle? I'm a fair to middling shot with a pistol, but that's no good for long range work.'

'Jake, the man I was travelling with, he'd a rifle. It's laying yonder, beneath him. You want I should fetch it?'

'If you ain't too squeamish 'bout touching a dead body, I reckon that's a right smart scheme.'

'Squeamish? Is that what you think o' me?' She

marched over to one of the bodies, reached under it and produced a military carbine, which she took back to Harker, along with a cartridge pouch which she had detached from the dead man's belt. Lord, thought Harker to himself, but you're a cold-blooded one and no mistake.

The riders had halted some half mile off and looked as though they were minded to hold the road against anybody trying to make their way onwards, in the general direction of Missouri. Even at this distance, they had an air about them which put Jed Harker in mind of soldiers, rather than bandits. He couldn't have said why he felt this, other than that he had himself been in the military for a spell and there was an indefinable something about those three riders. He turned to Abigail Tyler and said, 'Time to stop fooling around. You want my help, you best tell me what's afoot, or I swear to God I'm like to dig up and leave you. What's going on?'

'I've got something they want.'

'I don't know how slow you think I am, Miss Tyler, but I'd just about figured that out for my own self.'

'Well then, those men are working for some politicians in Richmond. Away down in Virginia, you know.'

Jed Harker glanced at the three riders, who were still immobile, like they might be posing for some statue, and said, 'If so, then they're a long way out of their jurisdiction. What authority can they have out here in Arkansas?'

13

'It's by way of being a long story, but these men aim to take what I have in this wagon and me too, unless I miss my guess.' Seeing the look of horror which came into Harker's eyes at the idea of a woman being snatched for carnal purposes, she laughed shortly and said, 'They don't want my body. They're more interested in what's in my head. We don't have time to talk on that. Will you help me or no?'

'Well, I won't desert you. Let's hope those boys are open to reason.'

It was typical of Jed Harker that he should have it in mind to reason, rather than to fight. He had had his fill of shooting and killing and since leaving the army, and always tried to find a way of solving difficulties which did not entail violence and bloodshed. He said, 'What if we raised a flag o' truce and tried to talk with them?'

'Wouldn't o' thought it'd do a mort of good, but if you think it's worth trying, then go ahead.'

The experiment was, however, destined never to be essayed, for at that moment a musket ball struck the side of the wagon; not a foot from where Harker was resting his hand. He said, 'The murderous rogues, they mean to kill us!'

'So I calculated,' said the woman imperturbably. 'They've figured you and me are surplus to requirements.'

Harker was already crouching down, behind the wagon. Abigail Tyler joined him. He said, 'What

14

weapon do you have, Miss Tyler?'

'Muzzle loader,' she replied, reaching for the gun she had placed in the wagon while they had unloaded the crates. 'You got Jake's carbine and that's a breech loader.'

'To be sure,' said Harker. He had slung the rifle carelessly on his back, with the strap across his chest when Abigail had handed it to him. Now he lifted it over his head and took the pouch from where he had placed it in the inside pocket of his jacket. It contained half a dozen glazed linen cartridges. He opened the breech and slipped one of the tubes of powder in and checked that the pellet primer was charged. Then he cocked the hammer and said to the woman, 'They fired on me, which makes this my dispute, whatever it is you're up to.'

He risked a peep over the top of the wagon and saw that the three riders were moving in slowly. The carbine could be sighted to half a quarter mile, but those men were half that distance; if that.

'You know how to handle it?' asked the woman dubiously. 'It's only come out less than a year ago.'

'It's a Sharps. I used the model they made in '55. This ain't all that different. You want to load and get ready to give fire? Or you want to gossip about my knowledge o' weaponry?'

From somewhere about her person, Abigail Tyler produced a powder-horn and also a small pewter box from which she took a ball and cap. Then she loaded the long musket.

Harker said, 'You've no wadding. Be sure not to let that thing droop or your ball will be running out.'

'You tend to your own affairs, mister. We going to start this or what?'

'I reckon,' said Harker and stood up. He rested the barrel of the Sharps on the side of the wagon and took careful aim. The shot flew straight and true, taking the middle rider slap-bang in the chest. At almost the same moment, the woman fired as well. Her shot didn't strike either of the other two riders, who began firing back at them; one with a pistol and the other with a carbine similar to the one which Harker was himself wielding.

The fellow with the pistol could be disregarded at that range; it was the rifleman who would need to be taken down. All the advantage was with the defenders, who in the first place were firing from cover and in the second were on the ground, rather than horseback. Harker reached into the pouch for another cartridge, but as he opened the breech of the Sharps and popped it in, Abigail Tyler's musket barked again, and Harker observed the pistoleer's horse rear up and throw its rider. He held his fire to see what would happen next and was mightily pleased when the remaining rider turned tail and began cantering off in the direction from which he'd come. He was followed by the loping figure of the man who'd had his horse shot out from under him.

Harker turned to the woman and said, 'I'm

16

damned if you didn't reload that muzzle-loader faster than I could get another cartridge in this thing, if you'll forgive the language.'

She laughed, saying, 'I grew up the only girl in a passel of boys. I could shoot and ride sooner than I could walk almost.' Then she said, 'I'm sorry if I was a bit rough. I'm really very grateful for your help.'

'I don't know but what you wouldn't have managed well enough without my help. You strike me as one who knows how to take care of herself.'

When the oxen were harnessed back to the wagon, and the crates stowed in it, there was no more reason to delay. Harker had been thinking and as he mounted up, he said, 'You got anybody to meet you wherever you're going?'

'I hope to hitch up with somebody a little further north.'

'Well then, I'll ride along of you for a spell. Maybe you can favour me with some explanation of what this is all about. I reckon you owe me that at the least.'

'That's right good of you. I don't think that you gave me your name.'

'It's Harker. Jed Harker. Folks mostly call me Jed.'

'Should we linger here? It may be as somebody heard the shooting.'

'You're right. Let's make our way on. I'm guessing that you're heading for Lovett? Leastways, there's nothing else along this track, less'n you're fixing to carry on straight to Missouri.'

17

'No, you're quite right. I'm on my way to Lovett. There's someone there I need to take counsel with.'

CHAPTER 2

As the oxen pulled the wagon north, Harker thought it would be right churlish to let a woman drive them and so he tethered the mare to the back of the cart and climbed up to take control of the slow-moving beasts which were hauling the wagon. He had never taken to oxen, which were among the slowest of God's creatures as well as being more stubborn and awkward than mules, into the bargain. At first, Harker used the whip freely, until he had established who was in charge. The pair of oxen then settled down to a leisurely pace, at least not stopping or attempting to leave the track, which was something. Once the cart was moving steadily, he said to the woman at his side, 'Time for some explaining. I been shot at and now I've killed a man, which some would consider a hanging matter. What's the game?'

'I've been travelling with a man who helped me make something. It's a piece of machinery that I'm taking north.'

'You'll pardon me for saying, ma'am, that that don't listen right. Why'd five men waylay you and start a gun battle over some bit of machinery? I'm strongly of the opinion that there's more to the case than that.'

'It doesn't matter what it is. It's useful and there's men in the south want it. Listen, you're not a supporter of slavery, are you?'

'What's that got to do with the price of sugar? I don't know that my views on anything is worth talkin' of.'

'That's where you're wrong,' said Abigail Tyler passionately. 'Coming the time when that's like to be the only opinion that matters. Meaning whether you're for or against it, that is to say.'

The truth was, Jed Harker didn't care over-much for being buffaloed into holding this view or that. He had managed to get through more than thirty years without holding, or expressing, any strong opinions. He didn't intend for this strange woman to start crowding him into agreeing to anything now, either. He said, 'Well, just as you say, Miss Tyler.'

The oxen had somehow sensed that Harker's attention had wandered from them and as a matter of course, began to slow down. He flicked them with the whip, to remind them that he was still in charge and the wagon began moving again, heading north along the road to Lovett. The excitement of the brief skirmish with the irregulars had livened up his journey a little, it was true. He hadn't seen such

action since the fighting in Mexico, but having freed
this peculiar woman from her foes, Harker felt no
further obligation towards her. He was mildly interested in her story, but then people oft-times lied and
he'd no occasion to think that she'd tell him the
unadorned truth. He'd more or less decided that she
wasn't really his type, with her fierce nature and
strong views. He was looking for peace and quiet, not
to get himself mixed up with a heap of politics.

For a man dead set on not becoming involved in
political matters nor admitting, even to himself, that
he was possessed of any definite views on the subjects
which so exercised the minds of those around him,
Jed Harker could hardly have chosen a worse place
than Lovett; a small town in the north of Arkansas,
just a few miles from the Missouri border. For one
thing, Lovett was one of the final stops on the so-
called Underground Railroad, which spirited away
escaped slaves to the north, where they could find
refuge in either Canada or some of the more enlight-
ened territories of the United States, such as Iowa or
Nebraska. There were many people, even in the deep
south, who were disgusted at the very idea of slavery
and these individuals had banded together in a loose
association which sheltered runaways and escapees
and passed them from home to home, until they
could be delivered to safety in the north.

Lovett's connection with the underground railroad was one reason that the town was simmering
with tensions which lay just beneath the surface.

21

Another was the presence of troops who, although still ostensibly belonging to the armed forces of the United States, had already pledged their real allegiance elsewhere. Arkansas was of crucial strategic importance for those who hoped that one day the southern states might break free of Washington's control and form their own federation of slave-owning states; who knew, perhaps even a nation of their own? Giving, as it did, control of the Mississippi River, Arkansas would be a vital bulwark against interference from the government in Washington; should such a plan ever come to fruition. For this reason, troops commanded by officers devoted to the cause of Cotton, Slavery and States' Rights were already being brought up into Arkansas from the south in preparation for what some referred to as 'The Great Enterprise'. It was into the heart of this powder-keg that Jed Harker was heading on 5 March 1860. Living and working in the interior of the state, he had not really seen much of the frenzied activity which now gripped the northern part of Arkansas.

They reached Lovett a little before sunset and it did not take long for Harker to come to the conclusion that here was a town in the posture of war. He looked around uneasily, as he noticed that while some of the troops looked like regular forces, others were clearly from militia units. He said to Abigail Tyler, 'I don't know what's up here, but were I you, I'd cut your stay in this town as short as can be. If what you're hinting at has any foundation and there are men in the south who want that invention of yours, then I'd say offhand that it won't take 'em long to acquire it if you hang around here for more than a day or so.'

'What do you advise we should do?'

'I don't advise nothing, Miss Tyler. And there's no "we" in the case. This is where you and me part company.'

'You'd leave me now?'

'I've pulled your chestnuts out of the fire once, so to speak,' said Harker laconically. 'I ain't about to repeat the exercise. This here's where you and me wish each other farewell.' He halted the wagon and jumped down. Before going to the back of the cart to unhitch the mare, he said, 'I don't know what you propose, but were I you, I'd think long and hard on your next move. There's three dead men not so far from here and unless I miss my guess, their friends'll be wanting to call somebody to account. So long.'

For all Jed Harker knew to the contrary, this would be the last he would see of Miss Tyler. He was curious about the bits of her story which she'd not got around to covering, but not so curious that he wished to remain in her vicinity. He'd a notion that if some of the men currently in the neighbourhood of Lovett were to succeed in connecting him in any way with the shooting which had lately been perpetrated, then there wouldn't even be the semblance of a trial; he would just be strung up or shot, out of hand. As he strolled down the main street of Lovett, Harker's only thought was how soon he would be able to travel north. He found a livery stable which agreed to take care of the mare for as long as he wished and he paid for a night in advance. There was nothing really to connect him in anybody's mind with the shooting on the road south and as long as that strange woman kept her own mouth tightly closed, which she had every reason to do, then it was a hundred to one against anything ever coming of it.

It is not to be supposed that Jed Harker was an especially callous or unthinking man; it was more that he had not had any desire to kill anybody and when all was said and done, it was the other party who had first fired on him, putting him in fear of his life. His conscience was clear on the matter, but he was not sure how the thing might present itself to any relatives or friends of those who lay dead by the roadside; a short distance from this town. It was while he was mentally exculpating himself in this way that Harker stumbled upon a scene which was to have the most profound and lasting effect upon the course of his life for the next few weeks. Later, he cursed himself for his impulsiveness, but being the man he was, what happened had a kind of inevitability about it.

As has been already seen, Jed Harker was a man who would have scorned to decline aid to a woman who was in need. The other thing which he would not turn a blind eye to was any mistreatment of a child. So it was that when – as he was searching for a

24

place to spend the night – he happened to see a mean-looking man knocking a young boy about in the most brutal way, he felt compelled to stop and offer his views and opinions about such conduct. That the man was white and the boy black did not strike Harker either then or later as being in any way germane to the issue.

The boy who was being beaten was perhaps ten years of age and the man who had gripped his arm and was striking him repeatedly about the head and upper body was a swarthy fellow in early middle age, who had to Harker's eyes a military bearing, although he was dressed in civilian clothes. He was a very natty and fastidious dresser, by the look of him, for he was wearing an immaculate black suit which wouldn't have looked out of place on a clergyman. The brightly coloured cravat though, to say nothing of the gold earring, did not fit in well with the idea that this was a man of the cloth. Whatever the fellow's calling might have been, to Jed Harker's way of thinking, his conduct was that of a beast, rather than a civilized being. He walked straight up and said, 'You're a brave one, I don't think, knocking a child about. Care to try your luck on a grown man?'

The man glanced round and said, 'Tend to your own affairs, stranger. This black rascal belongs to me. I'll do as I please with him.'

'Belongs to you, hey?' said Harker. 'You think a man can own a child, the way he does a horse or a pair of boots? You've taken a wrong turn somewhere along the road. Maybe I need to set you on the right path.'

Relinquishing his hold on the boy, the man in the black suit stood up straight and turned to face Harker. The top of his head was only on a level with Harker's chin, which caused Jed Harker to suppose that things might be about to get a little lively. He had observed over the years that it was almost a law of nature that the shorter the man, the more apt was he to take affront and display aggression when he thought others were trying to shove him around.

'So,' said the little man, 'you think to meddle in my business, is it? You'd do better to stick your snout in a hornets' nest.'

Harker noticed that the man spoke with a faint, but perceptible accent; the word 'so' coming out more like 'zo'. French, he thought, Creole from Louisiana perhaps. He said, 'Ain't meddling in nobody's business, not nohow. Just advising you to let that child alone.'

Both the man and the boy were staring in astonishment at Harker, as though he were some species of natural curiosity. Passers-by on the boardwalk had also stopped and were listening attentively to the exchange. Jed Harker cursed himself for a fool and tried to adopt a reasonable and pacific tone. He said, 'I'm not looking for trouble, it's just that I don't like to see a child treated so. Since you stopped hitting him, there's no more to say. I'll be on my way.' He turned to leave, but the other man raised his voice

26

and spoke a few words for the edification of the bystanders who were now gathering to see what was happening.

'See here now,' said the man, 'here is an abolitionist, come to tell us all that we must not own slaves! These people have the pride of Lucifer that they come south to us and preach what we should do in our own state.'

One of the men watching from the boardwalk called out jocularly, 'Happen he's been reading that *Uncle Tom's Cabin* that all them northerners is so all-fired keen on!' This raised a laugh from the small crowd.

Somebody else said loudly, 'Damned abolitionists!'

It was Jed Harker's distinct impression that popular opinion was not on his side and since he had good reason for not wishing to draw too much attention to himself, he said, 'Sorry if I've caused any offence.' He made to walk off, but the man who had been beating the black boy was having none of it.

'Don't turn your back on me, you son of a whore. You interfere with me, tell us that slavery is wrong and then think to walk free. Not a bit of it.'

Harker turned to face the man and said quietly, 'What will you have? You want that we should brawl in the dirt like a pair o' guttersnipes?'

'I demand satisfaction.'

Even now, Jed Harker didn't twig the direction in which matters were now tending. Had he spent time in the deep south and lived somewhere like Georgia, he might have seen quicker where this was leading. He contented himself with saying, 'Well, like I said, I'm not looking for trouble. Why don't we leave it at that?'

'I don't think so. I am insulted. I demand that you meet me for an affair of honour.'

'Ah, tell me you don't mean for us to fight a duel?' said Harker, at last catching on. 'Surely that ain't needful?'

'I demand it.'

He had heard vaguely of such things, but the idea that in this year of grace 1860, anybody would challenge him, Jed Harker, to a duel, would never have crossed his mind for a moment. For a man who had hoped to spend a peaceful and unobtrusive day or two in this berg, he had somehow contrived to make himself the chief object of interest in the whole, entire place. He said, 'I'm no swordsman, if that's what you're a drivin' at.'

'You fire a pistol, no? I see you carry one.'

'You don't mean for us to fight a gun battle here in the highway?'

'No, I say that we should go out of the town a way and then see what we see. There will be seconds to ensure fair play. Or are you a coward, as well as a meddling dog of an abolitionist?'

'You're a pressing man. If you'll have it so, then so be it. When had you in mind?'

'Night is drawing on. Tomorrow. Dawn is the proper hour for such things to be settled.'

Harker weighed things up in his mind. At length, he said, 'I'm fixin' to stay at that hotel over yonder. You want, you can send word there later and say when and where. But I hope you'll think better of it. I'd as soon shake hands here and now and be done with it.'

'My second will call upon you this night.'

With that, the elegant little Frenchman turned on his heel and strode off along the street. The little black boy glanced quickly at Harker, as though hoping to memorize his features, and then went trotting off after his master.

It was pretty plain to Harker that being taken for an abolitionist in this town was not the best character in which to appear. The looks he received when he nodded to the loafers and other interested parties who had congregated on the boardwalk to watch his confrontation with the man whose name he didn't even know, were not returned. Instead, he was met with hard stares. It was obvious that anything approaching abolitionist tendencies was not going to be welcome in this district.

The town's only hotel consisted of a dozen rooms in the upper storeys of the Last Post saloon. He had no difficulty obtaining a room for the night and went down to see about getting hold of some vittles. Almost the first person he saw in the dining room, which was really no more than a cordoned off section of the saloon, was Abigail Tyler. She was standing near the dining room and greeted him a little coldly.

'I didn't expect to see you here, Mr Harker.'

'Likewise. You're staying here as well?'

'Well, there's seemingly nowhere else.'

The man who doubled as both cook and waiter saw that his only two customers apparently knew each other. Seeing a chance to save on time by preparing one table, rather than two, he bustled over and said, 'Say, you two are friends, right? Know what, how'd it be were I to set you both at the same table in this corner? It's fine and private and you won't be troubled by any of those rough types drinking in the bar room.'

Giving them no opportunity to object to the arrangement, he ushered them over to a table in a darkened part of the room, which might have suited two young lovers looking for a *tête à tête*, but was hardly what either Jed Harker or Abigail Tyler wanted.

When they were seated, the woman said in a bright and sarcastic tone, 'Well, ain't this cosy?'

'Yes,' said Harker, not wishing to appear disagreeable, 'it's just the very thing.'

They had hardly settled themselves at their table, when a grave-looking man in his middle years walked across from the bar-room and presented his card to Harker, saying, 'Have I the honour to be addressing the man who crossed paths with my comrade, Claude Chappe?'

'I didn't catch his name, but if you refer to him as I lately had an altercation with in the highway, then yes, I reckon as it's me you're looking for.'

'Monsieur Chappe begs me to say that he will meet you tomorrow at dawn to settle the differences subsisting between you and he which led to his being insulted. Have you a second who will act for you?'

'Have I a what?'

'A second, one who will attend you and see that the proprieties are observed.'

'Proprieties?' exclaimed Harker in amusement. 'I'm going to fight the man, not court him with a view to matrimony.'

'Ah, you have a sense of humour,' said the man whose card declared him to be Colonel Quinnell, 'I like that. One of my fellow officers might perhaps be prevailed upon to undertake the office. You might not know the town. One of my colleagues will attend upon you tomorrow at, say, five in the morning, to conduct you to the location.'

'That sounds just fine and dandy, Colonel. I shall look forward to it.'

Colonel Quinnell bowed gracefully and left. Abigail Tyler looked dumbstruck at the proceeding and said, 'Lordy, you've been going it some. You've not been here more than an hour and already you fallen out with somebody. You goin' to be killed?'

'I wouldn't have thought so,' said Jed Harker soberly, 'although one never can tell.'

When the cook had returned and given them to understand the very limited range of comestibles on offer, Harker was prevailed upon by his companion to give a brief account of the incident which had led to his being challenged to fight a duel the next day. As he summed up the case, 'It's a heap o' foolishness. Little men always are on the scout for trouble. I seed it a hundred times. Lord preserve me from a bantam cock!'

'But you risk your life like this for that boy. I thought you weren't an abolitionist?'

'I don't need some fancy word to tell me what's right and what's wrong,' said Harker shortly. 'Fellow was knocking about a child and tellin' me that he owned him. That ain't right and there's an end to it. Don't try and draw me into some political business, Miss Tyler, for it won't answer. I'm a plain man, I have no time for politics or religion.'

There was some further desultory conversation during the meal, from which Harker gathered that the ox cart and its cargo would be heading north in another day or so. Abigail Tyler made no attempt to persuade him to join her on the journey, for which Harker was thankful. He made an excuse and turned in as soon as the meal was over. If he was really going to be called upon to fight for his life the following morning, then he'd better try and be as fresh as possible.

CHAPTER 3

Fortunately, for such an occasion as this, Jed Harker had from childhood been an early riser. When there was a pressing and particular reason for waking a little earlier than usual, he had only to tell himself so before falling asleep, and he would awaken at the required hour. So it proved that day, because he opened his eyes a little before half past four, when it was still pitch black outside the window.

Although he had been mixed up in his share of gunfights, a formal duel was something new in Harker's experience and he wondered how it would be arranged. He had his Navy Colt, but then again, he'd a notion that such a weapon would not be fitting for a proper duello of this nature. Well, he would just have to see what was what.

Downstairs, there was only a kitchen-boy at work and he was astonished to see one of the guests up and about at such an hour. When he caught sight of Harker, he said, 'Ain't no food served 'til seven or thereabouts, sir.'

'I'm not looking to eat,' Harker told him, 'but if you've such a thing as a cup of coffee to be had, I'll be eternally in your debt.'

Because this guest didn't appear to be one for standing on ceremony, the boy invited him into the kitchen and the two of them sat companionably at a table, supping sweet, black coffee.

'You got work to do this early?' the youth, who couldn't have been above fourteen years of age, asked Harker.

'In a manner of speaking. Fellow has it in mind to kill me.'

'Surely you're funning with me?'

'Not a bit of it,' Harker assured him cheerfully, 'I'm invited to what they call a duel, which is a novelty for me, I'll admit.'

'You ain't scared?'

'Of being killed? Man says as he's not affeared o' death at such a time is either a liar or a mad fool. I don't want to die more than the next man.'

'You could run away,' suggested the boy. 'Not fight, I mean.'

At that moment, there was the sound of footsteps in the bar-room outside and a moment later Colonel Quinnell appeared in the doorway to the kitchen. Harker winked at the boy and said, 'I'm obliged to you for the suggestion, son, but happen it's too late to act on it.' He got to his feet and said to the Colonel, 'I only have my pistol. Will that serve the purpose?'

Colonel Quinnell smiled and said, 'Monsieur Chappe has a pair of duelling pistols. I fancy they'll be better suited than a six-shooter.'

Before he and the Colonel left, Harker said to the boy, 'Bar I ain't been killed by then, I'll see you for breakfast, son.'

As the two of them strolled along the deserted main street, Harker could see that the sky in the east had a pale bluish tinge to it, which presaged dawn. He said to the man at his side, 'Your friend Chappe make a habit of this kind of thing? Meaning fighting duels?'

'Oh yes,' said the other sombrely, 'most every town we fetch up, somebody falls foul of him. Charleston, Atlanta, Baton Rouge; you name it, Claude Chappe has fought men there. Killed them too.'

'Well, you're a regular Job's comforter,' said Harker sourly and they continued on their way in silence.

Some half mile from Lovett's last building, they came to a little wood. On making their way through it, the two men emerged into a long clearing. By now, the sky was rosy pink and it wasn't long to sun-up. Colonel Quinnell said, 'We try to keep such affairs as this from prying eyes, you understand. That's why we choose this hour and place.'

In the gloom, Harker could make out three other people, besides he and the colonel. One of these was the man he had accosted the previous day, who was looking very satisfied with himself. Presumably, he was confident of killing Harker. The two others were introduced as Captain Preston, who was there nominally as Harker's second, and an army surgeon whose name was not given. Not for the first time, it struck Harker that the town seemed to be crammed to bursting point with soldiers from the south. What they were all doing in this corner of Arkansas was a mystery.

Chappe and the other two men greeted Harker courteously and the Frenchman produced a brass-bound, wooden case, which he opened for Harker's inspection. Inside, nestling in crimson velvet were a beautiful pair of duelling pistols. Not really expecting an answer, Harker said, 'Lord a mercy, you carry these about with you wherever you go?'

'Why yes,' replied Chappe. 'One never knows when one might be subjected to insolence.'

'Are they loaded?' asked Harker, for want of anything else to say. It appeared that they were not and that this was to be undertaken in the presence of all interested parties, so that there could not later be accusations of foul practice. It occurred to Harker, although he didn't say so out loud, that any victim of sharp practice in a business like this would be unlikely to survive and complain about it.

The pistols were single-shot percussion-locks and judging by the size of the balls, had a calibre roughly the same as his own pistol, a 0.36. When both were charged, they were replaced in the box, which was then offered to Harker. This was, he supposed, another way of ensuring fair play. He selected one of the weapons without thinking too much of it. It fitted neatly in his grasp and he hefted it. The balance was perfect.

'Take your places, back to back, gentlemen,' said Colonel Quinnell. 'Then, at the signal, take ten paces and then turn and fire.'

As he walked to the middle of the glade, Harker wondered how much an event like this relied upon the honesty and good will of those involved. Was he supposed to walk those ten paces slowly? Stroll, like he was on a Sunday walk in the park? What if he should fairly race along and turn and fire before his opponent had yet finished his own ten paces?

As it was, when the signal was given, Jed Harker walked at his normal speed, counting carefully those ten paces. He felt that it would hardly be in the spirit of the thing to whirl around and fire from the hip; like he was in a shootout in a saloon. He stopped and turned slowly; only to find that Claude Chappe was already aiming his pistol straight at Harker. Before he could figure out whether the other man had – with the connivance of the supposed 'seconds' – taken fewer paces than himself and turned sooner, and if so, what he should do about it like raising his own gun right fast and firing at once, Chappe pulled the trigger.

There was a dull, metallic click, signifying a misfire. The pistols used the same copper caps as his own to detonate the charge. These were smeared on the inside with fulminate of mercury and fitted over a nipple which had a hollow tube leading down to the charge of gunpowder. Sometimes, generally because the manufacturing process was inefficient, a cap came through and was sold which had no fulminate in it. This was evidently what had happened to Chappe.

Without any hesitation, Jed Harker raised his pistol and pointed it directly at Chappe. Then he lowered it and fired into the ground between them. A shower of dirt and stones was flung up, some of which hit the little Frenchman. Harker said, 'I've no wish to kill a man in cold blood over a trifling quarrel. I reckon as honour is satisfied on both sides.'

The other four men stared at him strangely, as though baffled and frustrated. He knew then that his suspicions had been correct and there had been a conspiracy to allow Chappe to murder him by turning and aiming before he had even finished walking. He transferred the duelling pistol to his left hand and then drew the revolver from his belt; cocking it with his thumb as he did so. None of the others moved.

Setting Chappe's fancy pistol down on the ground, while never once taking his eyes off the others, gave Harker time to think of what he would next say and do. Facing the other men, he delivered himself of the following sentiments.

'You're a set of cowards and scallywags. You make

much of your "affairs of honour" and suchlike, but you ain't got a morsel of honour between the whole bunch of you. But for that misfire, you woulda let that little brute shoot me down. I was lured out here to be killed and you had it all guyed up so folk'd think it was a fair fight. Disgusting!' He backed slowly into the trees of the wood, his gun pointing all the time in the direction of the four men. Only when he was clear of the wood did he turn around and walk briskly back to town.

As he walked to Lovett, Harker pondered on what had just befallen him. At first, he wondered if this had been some revenge for the men he had killed yesterday, but he didn't think that likely. Why go through all this charade if his part was known, concerning the two recent deaths in which he'd had a hand? No, the neatest solution was the simplest. Chappe was presumably their friend and they were happy to oblige him by helping him to kill those who crossed him. The fact that he was a northerner who had been expressing vociferously his disapproval of slavery had perhaps not endeared him to them either. They were southrons and probably diehard adherents of the cause; believers in the sanctity of cotton, slavery and states' rights. His few choice words yesterday on the impossibility of a man owning other fellow humans must have struck at the heart of all that they held most dear. Well, be damned to them! He would be leaving the town that very day and they could get up to whatever games they chose.

He had had an interesting and profitable time running that livery stable, but things in this part of the state were a little too lively for his taste.

It was only just light and there still weren't many people on the streets. Harker thought he could do with a bite to eat and went back to the hotel. The boy with whom he had had a coffee was pleased to see him and eager to hear of all that had happened since he had gone off with Colonel Quinnell. It seemed to Jed Harker that he had not been expected back alive and that there was a certain novelty value about his return. He could not help but wonder if other men had been led on to fight rigged duels with the man called Chappe and if so, for what purpose. One thing was for certain, there was a lot more going on here than could be seen on the surface. Not that it mattered really, because he would be out of Lovett in just a few hours.

At seven, Jed Harker ate a good breakfast and then went out to see if any of the stores were opening yet, so that he could acquire some provisions for his journey north to Missouri. One provisions store was open and he went in to buy some bread and cheese, which would serve him well enough for a day or two on the road. Although it was so early, there were already a few customers in the place. Two troopers in uniform were standing and chatting amiably to the storekeeper. They fell silent when Harker approached the counter and stared at him coldly. Once again, Harker couldn't make out why there were so many military in and about the town. Not that it mattered to him. He said, 'Do you have a loaf or two of bread that I could buy, please?'

'Don't sell to Jayhawkers,' said the old man behind the counter.

'I'm sorry, I don't rightly understand you,' said Harker in bewilderment, 'I just want some bread.'

'Yes, but you see, your custom ain't wanted here,' said the man.

One of the soldiers stepped forward towards Harker and said, 'Don't you hear good, mister? Man says as he won't be sellin' you nothing.'

Perplexed by the attitude of the men, Jed Harker could think of no fitting response and so mumbled an apology and left the store. He walked up and down Main Street for half an hour, until another store opened and then tried there, with the same result. The owner said flatly, 'I don't need your custom. I got my business to consider.'

All this was very puzzling and Harker scarcely knew what to make of it. He mulled the question over in his mind and the only thing he was able to come up with was that his views on slavery, expressed in the public highway the previous day, had been voiced abroad and were sufficient in themselves to render his presence unwelcome in the town. But that sounded crazy. He'd only said that he didn't think that a man could own fellow beings, surely to God that was a sensible enough point of view? It shouldn't be enough to brand him a pariah! It was while he was trying to unravel this thread, that Harker became aware of a man walking alongside him, somebody who apparently desired conversation with him. He gauged this, because the man said in an undertone, hardly moving his lips, 'Don't look round at me. Just keep walking, like you haven't even noticed me. Now turn to your right and the two of us can slip down the space there, between those two buildings.'

Jed Harker was not so green that he was about to enter a secluded space with a total stranger. His hackles were already up, following the events of the last twenty-four hours and so he turned to look closely at the fellow who had invited him to go down the alleyway. He saw a man of sixty or more, with snow-white hair and a neatly trimmed beard to match. He was soberly dressed and there was a look of benevolence and good humour on his ruddy face. He looked like a prosperous farmer or rancher. If Jed Harker was any judge of men, then this was an innocuous and trustworthy individual. He accordingly followed him into the space between the hardware store and corn chandler. The man led him all the way along, until the two of them emerged onto an empty lot where nobody else was to be seen.

'What's to do?' asked Harker bluntly.

'You're to do, my boy!' replied the old man jovially. 'Why, you're the theme of universal conversation.'

'I can't imagine why.'

'Can you not, Mr Harker? You surprise me.'

'How come you know my name, Mr. . . ?'

'Jackson,' said the man, thrusting out his hand, 'Abednego Jackson.' After they had shaken hands, he continued, 'As for how I know your name, we have a mutual friend.'

'I'm blessed if I know who that might be. I've never been in this town before. Don't aim to return once I've left, for the matter of that.'

'It's no mystery. Her name is Abigail Tyler. She tells me that she fell in with you on the road yesterday.'

Jed Harker's heart sank at these words. Had that wretched woman been voicing it abroad that he had killed a heap of men just lately? As if things weren't tricky enough as they stood! He said, 'Miss Tyler's nothing to do with me. What is it you want?'

'We can't talk here. There's a chance of being overheard. Why don't you walk out to my house? It's only a mile from the edge of town.'

'If this is something to do with Miss Tyler, then I'd as soon not. I mean to be out of here by midday.'

The old man suddenly looked very angry. His eyes flashed and his beard bristled, as he said in a ringing tone, 'This has no reference to Abigail Tyler. I'm talking about your own soul, man.' His fiery way of speaking made the man look like an Old Testament prophet. Harker was about to interrupt, but seeing this, the old fellow raised a hand to ward him off, saying, 'I was there yesterday when you made yourself so unpopular in this town by preaching your detestation of slavery. They've taken you for some

43

abolitionist agitator, you know. Just the kind of person they least want to see in these parts.'

'They got me muddled up with another.'

'Indeed? Did I not hear you say with your own lips that it was not possible for a man to own another person like he did a horse or a pair of boots?'

Harker shifted uncomfortably and said, 'If I did, what then?'

'Was it just bluster and brag, or did you mean what you said?'

'I meant it right enough.'

'Good. Then come along of me to my house and we'll reason the matter out together.'

It has to be said that Jed Harker did not receive this invitation with any great enthusiasm, but felt in some way as though he had been hoisted by his own petard. It was true that he had voiced the opinions attributed to him, but that didn't mean that he had any desire to act upon them. He wanted only to leave this wretched little town and move on north to more civilized districts.

Abednego Jackson lived in a large wooden farmhouse about a mile and a half from the edge of town. The house was surrounded by perhaps thirty acres of cultivated land, but it looked to Harker barely enough to maintain a man. Not all the fields which he could see were presently under the plough and yet Jackson looked as though he were living pretty comfortably off. There was something here that did not altogether add up.

Near to the house was a barn and it was to here that Jackson first led his guest, which seemed to Harker a little odd. Jackson, perhaps guessing what the other man was thinking, turned to him and said, 'We'll go in the house later. I want to show you something first.' As they approached the barn, Jackson called out, 'Don't be afeared, Jemima, it's only me.'

Before Harker could work out what was going on, a young black woman appeared at the entrance to the barn. She was carrying a baby in her arms and looked terrified out of her wits. Jackson said, 'Don't fret, child. It's almost time for you to move out. This gentleman is going to assist you.'

'The devil I am!' exclaimed Jed Harker. 'What do you mean by telling her so? What game are you about here?' Then realization struck him and he said, 'Tell me you're not part o' this here underground railroad that I hear tell of? There's men been hanged for that, by vigilance men. What do you think you're about, trying to draw me in on this?'

The black woman, who looked to be no more than twenty-five years of age, looked at him fearfully, as though she thought that he meant her harm. He said, 'Sorry if I sounded a mite rough, miss, but I been inveigled into this unwitting like, and I don't aim to get mixed up in such goings on. But I won't inform on you or nothin', you can rest easy on that score.'

'It'll be fine, Jemima, just you and your little one rest a little longer and then we'll see about eating.'

'Thank you, Mr Jackson, suh.'

'How many times must I tell you, not "sir". Just call me Abednego.' He turned to Harker and said, 'Come into the house now and we'll visit some more with Jemima later.'

Once they were out of earshot of the woman, Jed Harker said hotly, 'That's a scurvy trick to play on that girl, tellin' her as I'm a going to be helpin' of her. Why're you raising her hopes so?'

Jackson opened the kitchen door and Harker followed him in. As he had already noticed, there was evidence of considerably more money than that likely to be generated by the sparsely cultivated fields around the house. Looking around, Harker guessed that here was the home of a man with independent means of some kind. As he busied himself lighting the stove and setting a pot of coffee on it, Jackson said, 'You'll take a cup of coffee with me, Mr Harker? Then I'll lay all my cards down and we can both see where we stand.'

Not wishing to sound ungracious, Harker said quietly, 'You'll find I'm not apt to change my mind, but I'll hear what you have to say.'

'I reckon that's all I could ask.'

One they were settled companionably at the table, Abednego Jackson said, 'I'm guessing you know how things are situated. There are slaves trying to flee to the north every day. Some of us help them. I'm a Quaker, so it's kind of a duty to me. Things are getting dangerous though and with the fighting up in Kansas between the abolitionists and those who'd vote Kansas into being a slave state, we can't send anybody through Missouri, like we've been doing 'til now.'

'That's all very interesting, but I don't see that it concerns me in the least degree.'

'That woman, Jemima, escaped with her child. Soon as the child can walk, her owners would be selling it on to somebody. They're breeding women like cattle or horses. It's an abomination.'

'I kind o' agree with you, but I'd as soon not get mixed up in it.'

Harker stopped talking and listened carefully. In the distance, he could hear hoofbeats and if he was any judge, then they were heading this way. He said, 'You expecting company?'

'Why yes. Two friends of yours.'

Thoroughly perplexed, Jed Harker got to his feet and went over to the door. Some way off, he could see an ox-drawn wagon moving slowly towards the house. He guessed immediately that this would be Abigail Tyler and her mysterious cargo. Presumably this was one of the 'friends' to whom Jackson had alluded, but Harker could not for the life of him imagine who the second might be. As the wagon came within hailing distance, Abigail Tyler called out, 'Well, I didn't think I'd be seeing you again, Mr Harker.'

Under his breath, Harker muttered, 'I wouldn't have thought it likely myself.' Then, in a louder voice, he called back, 'Good day to you, Miss Tyler.'

Then, when the wagon pulled up outside the house, Harker received two shocks in quick succession. The first was when a head emerged from the canvas covering the crates at the back of Abigail Tyler's wagon. It was the boy whose ill-treatment had caused Harker to become embroiled in the duel that morning. He was just getting over the surprise of this, when the young black woman came running out of the barn, shouting joyfully. The boy jumped down from the wagon and ran to her, whereupon she embraced him, clutching him tight, as though she never wanted to let him go. As he watched her kiss the boy's face and run her fingers through his kinky hair, Harker was left in no doubt that this must be another child of Jemima's.

Jackson came up softly behind Harker and said quietly, 'Ain't that something to see? She's been parted from that boy of hers for nearly a year, since her master sold him to that swaggering little Frenchman that you fell foul of.'

'You're a rare scoundrel,' said Harker. 'You thought once I'd seen this, I wouldn't be able to walk away from that proposal of yours, is that the strength of it?'

'Pretty well,' admitted the other man, who had at least the grace to look a little abashed. 'Well, can you? Meaning, can you walk away now?'

'What's the story behind this?'

'A common enough one in slave states like this.

48

When the boy was nine, the master needed some ready cash-money and so he sold him. His mother was heart-broken. She'd a little 'un by then and was plumb distracted. Six months back, me and some friends set a plan going to reunite 'em and send them north. That's it and as you see, we're ready to proceed.'

Jed Harker hated the idea of that boy and his mother, to say nothing of the baby, setting off with no protector. He said, 'What's the idea, head straight up into Missouri?'

'Can't be done. There's skirmishing up there on the line 'tween Missouri and Kansas. They'll have to go through the Indian Nations and come into Kansas from the south.'

'I don't take to being buffaloed into doing things, Mr Jackson. I'd have you recollect that another time. It sits ill with me.'

'Why, my boy, who's buffaloing you? Just walk away now, if you've a mind to.'

'I'm going back into town. All else apart, my horse is there. I need to think on this matter.'

Harker didn't want to speak to the runaway slaves or even look them in the eye. It would make it all the harder if he did decide to avoid having anything to do with this mad scheme. He simply turned on his heel, nodded to Abigail Tyler, and trudged back to Lovett.

Once back in town, Jed Harker began to think that he must have been bewitched by Abednego Jackson and his crazy notions. What did any of this have to do with him, anyway? He felt sorry for that Jemima and her children, sure, but when all was said and done, it was no affair of his. Of a sudden, his mind was made up; they could all of them go hang! He'd collect the mare from the livery stable and be on his way. A mite rough up on the Kansas-Missouri border, was it? Well, he'd been in some scrapes before now and he doubted that it would be near as dangerous as the Mexican War had been.

It was pleasant to have made a firm decision and as he sauntered along Lovett's main street, Harker was feeling pretty braced with himself. That was until he reached the livery stable and learned that his horse was missing. The owner shrugged and said nonchalantly, 'Must have been stole in the night. Nothin' I can do about it.'

'The hell d'ye mean, it's nothing to do with you? I paid you to care for the beast. You've a duty under law. Don't fool with me now, I was running a livery stable myself until just lately. I know the law.'

The man laughed at that and said, 'So take me to law. Nearest courthouse is in Little Rock, forty miles as the crow flies. Good luck with it.'

'You son of a bitch,' began Harker, but noticed that two other men had emerged from the nearby outbuildings and were watching him. It struck him that the disappearance of the mare might well be connected with the fact that the folk in this town had him pegged for an abolitionist and after his little run-in with that fellow Chappe, they were hinting that they didn't care over much for Jed Harker or his opinions. There was nothing to be done. He said, 'I suppose those villains didn't make off with my saddle as well?'

'Why no,' said the livery stable owner, with a smirk, 'it's right in here for you to take away.'

There is something irresistibly comic about the sight of a seasoned rider who is compelled to go on foot for any distance, particularly when he is also obliged to carry his saddle and roll along of him. Harker could hear the snickers as he left the vicinity of the livery stable and made his way back down main street. This was, he thought, the hell of a thing to befall him.

CHAPTER 4

The loss of the mare had thrown all Jed Harker's schemes and plans plumb out of kilter. That he looked like a fool, walking down the street with the awkward burden of the saddle causing him to resemble a hunchback, was a minor consideration. He might just be able to scrape up enough to buy a horse, but he'd a strong suspicion that none of the local people here would be inclined to sell him one. It was while he was brooding in this way that Harker looked up straight into the eyes of Claude Chappe. He was glad to observe that Chappe's smart clothes were still a little besmeared with the dirt which had flown up when Harker had discharged his pistol into the ground between them, not five hours since. Chappe was standing outside a store, watching him approach. He was glowering and looked seriously angry. Harker wondered if Chappe had discovered yet that his boy was on the run. He nodded amiably at the Frenchman, and was unable to avoid saying in a friendly enough way, 'Lordie, that suit of yours could do with a thorough cleaning. It's covered all over with mud.' It may have been childish of him, but the look on Chappe's face as he made this helpful observation was priceless.

'You think that we are finished, you and me?' said Chappe. 'But no, it is not so. I will have your head yet.'

Harker stopped and placed the saddle on the ground. He said, 'I'd have you recall to mind that I spared your life. I could've killed you, all I did was muss up your clothes a little.'

From his expression, it didn't look as though Claude Chappe was all that pleased to be reminded of this. Maybe, thought Harker, he was one of that brand who rated his dignity higher than his life and would rather have been shot than covered in filth. Out loud, he said, 'You have anything you want to have out with me, Chappe, I'm standing here before you right now, ready and willing. I don't need no seconds, nor no other sort of fuss. You want to fight me now, man to man with fists or guns, just you say the word.'

At the mention of guns, one or two loafers who were standing outside the store and near to Chappe, moved off casually, as though they had just remembered that they had important business to attend to elsewhere. Harker stared at the other man and said, 'I don't aim for to be shot in the back. Come down now into the roadway and let's see what chances.'

For a moment, it looked as though Chappe might be about to take him up on the offer, for he drew himself up to his full, negligible height. Then, just when Harker was sure that he was about to step off the boardwalk and come down to face him, the Frenchman turned on his heel and walked off. Harker continued to stand there for a few seconds, feeling uncommonly foolish. Then he picked up his saddle and headed out of town towards Abednego Jackson's house.

Jackson did not seem to be overly surprised to see Jed Harker fetch up again at his house. He was pottering about, doing something to Abigail Tyler's wagon, when he saw Harker approaching. He hailed him cheerfully, crying, 'So you've a mind to join the little expedition after all, Mr Harker. I'm sure we're all obliged to you.'

Never one for dissembling, Harker filled the other man in on the lamentable loss of his mount. Jackson said, 'I've no doubt it's as you suspect. Somebody in town has made off with the horse to inconvenience you as a reprisal for your unwelcome views on the subject of slavery.'

'Inconvenience me?' said Harker. 'That's a charitable way of putting it. Some of the territories I passed through, stealing horses is a hanging matter.'

Jackson chuckled and said, 'You've a right dry sense of humour, you know that?'

Before he was able to frame a reply, Harker found that something or somebody was tugging at his

54

sleeve. He turned to see the black boy, with whom all this difficulty had begun, standing at his side. He said, 'You all right there, son? Is there aught I can do for you?'

'I wanted to thank you, sir. For what you done.'

'There's no "sir" in the case. My name's Jed, you can call me that. As for what I done, as God he knows, it was little enough. I never could abide a bully.'

'My ma, she wants to speak with you too.'

'Well,' said Harker, 'here I stand. Let her come over.'

The boy looked embarrassed and dug his toe in the ground, looking down at it as he did so. He said, 'She don't like to push herself forward, sir. She's over yonder in the barn.'

When Harker went over to see her, he found Jemima fussing with her youngest child. He said, 'What's to do, ma'am?'

'You saved my boy. I thank you for it.'

'It's kind of you to say so, but I didn't save your boy from nothin'. Just spoke a few words to the fellow as was troubling him. It was nothing.'

'It was everything,' said the woman, searching Harker's face. 'Is it true that you're going to take us north?'

'That,' said Harker, 'is what you might call a tricky point. It's certainly beginning to look that way. I hope you wouldn't object to me as a travelling companion?'

'I'd feel safe if you was with me, else not.'

'Well, let's see what happens, ma'am. Forgive me,
I needs must speak a few words to your host.'

Abednego Jackson was deep in conversation with
Abigail Tyler. Harker went up to them and said, 'If I
consent to ride on this little expedition, I want to
know what's in those crates in the back o' your
wagon, Miss Tyler.'

'It's nothing to do with you,' she said indignantly.
'Let's just say it's something which might stop this
trouble brewing with the north dead in its tracks.'

'I won't have any part in this, less'n I know what
I'm getting into,' said Harker firmly. 'It'd be bad
enough being caught assisting runaway slaves, but if
you're running guns to the Indians or something, I'll
have no part in it.'

Before the woman was able to reply, Jackson said
sharply, 'Hush now, the pair of you. I can hear
horses.' He shouted, 'Get in the barn and hide,
Pompey. Run now. Tell your ma to get up into the
hay loft and not to make a blessed sound.'

The boy needed no second bidding, but scooted
off at once. Jackson too turned on his heel and
walked into the house, leaving Harker and Abigail
Tyler to see what might develop. A slight rise of land
obscured the town of Lovett from view, even though
it was barely a mile away, but now Harker too could
hear hoofbeats coming from that direction. He
made sure that the pistol was loose in his belt and
was not overly surprised when Abigail reached into

56

her wagon and lifted out the same rifle which she had fired at Harker the previous day. He said, 'Don't start any shooting, you hear what I tell you? Like as not, whoever's heading this way is nothing to do with us.'

When the riders crested the rise of ground though, he saw that there were three of them. One was Claude Chappe and the other two were Colonel Quinnell and Captain Preston. Harker muttered under his breath, 'This is apt to be awkward.'

The three men reined in a dozen yards from Harker and the woman. Chappe said, 'I see you everywhere.'

'Well, I try to keep myself to myself,' said Harker apologetically, 'but you have a point, we do seem to keep bumping into one another. It's a small world.'

'My boy's been stolen,' said Chappe, 'you wouldn't know about that?'

'Stolen? Sure he ain't run away?'

'He would not dare. He knows I'd flay him alive.'

'You surely have a pleasant way with you, Chappe,' said Harker, staring at the other man in disgust. 'What's this to do with me, anyway? I don't have your boy.'

'I wasn't coming to find you. I heard that the man who moved here just lately is suspicioned. I think we'll search this place.'

Jed Harker walked closer to the three riders and said, 'This ain't my farm, but I'm not sure that I should give you permission to do that.'

There was still no sign of Jackson who, Harker supposed, was most likely hiding in his house. He glanced back and was relieved to see that Miss Tyler was holding her rifle loosely, as though she had just picked it up casually, to put in a cupboard or something. The hairs on the back of his neck were tickling and Harker knew that this was one of those occasions when making the wrong move or even using the wrong word, could lead to bloodshed.

Claude Chappe laughed, and the two men flanking him smiled too. He said, 'I wasn't looking for you to give me your permission. You and I still have business to conduct, don't press me to take it up with you now.'

'I've known a heap o' men like you in the past, Chappe. Bullies, full of bluster and showing off like little boys. I'm telling you now, you don't want to get crosswise to me.'

Chappe looked as though he could scarcely believe his ears. In a leisurely fashion, he reached forward and began pulling a short, military carbine from the scabbard which held it at the front of his saddle. Harker was torn between his instinctive desire to protect himself, by drawing his own weapon, and the hope that even at this late stage, bloodshed could be averted. He was saved from having to make any immediate decision, when a loud voice called, 'Pull that gun and you're as good as dead!'

The Frenchman froze at once and his two companions began casting their eyes around to see who had issued this challenge. It took a few seconds, but they eventually identified a rifle poking coyly out of one of the upper windows of the farmhouse. It was some fifty yards from them. They all realized almost at once that if it came to a shooting match, then the man firing from the shelter of the house would have the drop on them. This was before they noticed that Abigail Tyler had also raised the musket she was holding up to her shoulder and was now drawing down on them too. A quick murder, followed by a search of the property would have been one thing. A protracted gun battle between their party and an equal number of defenders though; that was another thing entirely.

Chappe opened his hand and let the rifle fall back, under its own weight, into the scabbard. He said loudly, so that the man at the window of the house would also be able to hear him, 'Don't anybody be hasty now. See, I have no weapon.'

'There's nothing for you here,' said Harker, trying to keep his voice calm and level. 'Were I you, I'd just turn around and ride back to town. That way, nobody'll get hurt.'

Claude Chappe glared at Harker and said, 'We'll go. For now.' Then he turned his horse and dug his spurs viciously into the beast's flanks. The two other men took a more leisurely departure, giving Harker and the woman the once-over, before leaving themselves.

When Jackson came out of the house, there was no sign of the rifle he'd poked out of the window. Harker said, 'I thought I understood you to say you was a Quaker. Ain't they opposed to bloodshed and war and suchlike?'

'Not if it's for the better good,' replied Abednego Jackson, with a wink. ''Sides which, I never said I was a perfect Christian. That's enough gossiping, those boys'll be back directly. You folk best be on your way. Abigail, there's baskets of victuals in the kitchen. Happen you could bring them here and stow 'em on your cart. Mr Harker, will you lend a hand to hitch up them oxen?'

There was ten minutes of bustling around, during the course of which Jemima and her children came out of hiding and stood, looking around uncertainly. When all was ready, Harker said, 'Well, I reckon I'm in on this game, whether or no. That little Frenchman wants my blood and so I might as well be doing something worthwhile while he hunts for me. You want I should drive those creatures?'

'I'd be eternally obliged to you, if you would,' said Abigail Tyler. 'They won't take a bit o' notice of me.'

Seeing that the black woman and her children looked a little lost, Harker went over and said, 'I shall be taking the reins, ma'am. I don't know if you or your boy would like to sit next to me or if Miss Tyler will wish to do so. Come over and join the deliberations afore we set out.' Jemima brought her two children over to where Abigail Tyler was standing

60

and engaged her in conversation in a low tone. It was not a quarter hour after Chappe and his companions had left, heading back towards Lovett, that the ox-cart began lumbering its way north towards the territories of the so-called 'five civilized tribes'.

Before they left, Jackson spoke privately to Jed Harker. He said, 'I don't doubt that the Lord will richly bless and reward you for undertaking this task, Mr Harker. From all that I am able to apprehend from Abigail – that is to say Miss Tyler – there is considerably more at stake than just the rescue of those poor souls who you're taking north. I don't know it all, but it might be that Abigail's enterprise is more important than just the lives of one or two people.'

'You're speaking in riddles,' said Harker, 'would you care to be more plain?'

'I think I'd best leave that to the lady herself.'

The wagon progressed at a maddeningly slow speed and even with the frequent application of the goad, Jed Harker was unable to coax the oxen into more than around five miles each hour. So leisurely was their pace, that Jemima and her son, walking alongside the wagon, outpaced it. Abigail Tyler, who was seated next to Harker, observed quietly, 'Jemima don't know what to make of you. She's uneasy.'

Harker looked round in amazement and said, 'I'm sure I don't know why. I treat her like everybody else. You ain't uneasy about me, I'm hopeful to think?'

'No, course not. But Jemima, she can't figure out why you call her ma'am and so on.'

61

'That's no mystery. I've not known her above a few hours. I only know her given name and I can't hardly take the liberty o' using that. I'd call any lady ma'am if I'd only known her a short while.'

'Well, it makes her feel strange. She's never had a white man speak so formal. Just call her Jemima, same as I do.'

'I'll tell you what, Miss Tyler,' said Harker, a little sharply, 'I don't need lessons in how to conduct myself from you. By the by, Mr Jackson gave me to understand that those crates of your'n have some importance. Now we're travelling together, perhaps you'd have the goodness to let me know what's in them?'

For a spell, it looked as though Abigail was minded to keep her own counsel, but at length she said, 'You ever use a sewing machine?'

'I ever use a what?' said Harker, thinking that he must have misheard.

'A sewing machine,' she said impatiently. 'You must have heard of them or even seen one. A needle goes up and down, very fast. You know what I'm talking about?'

'I seem to recollect hearing of some such, but I never seen one, let alone used it. Where is this tending? You sayin' you got sewing machines in those wooden boxes?'

'Don't be silly. So you never used one, is that right?'

'Do I look like a seamstress?'

62

'Not over-much. Here's the way of it. Some five years back, I invented a machine to do sewing. Fellow called Singer, away up north, he thought he'd got that line of machines pretty well tied up, but my one beat his hollow. I was in partnership with an engineer at that time and he dealt with that Singer, come to an arrangement. Singer bought me out and I had a tidy pile, me and my partner. I'm not goin' too fast for you, I suppose?'

'No, I ain't simple, for all that I've not had much in the way of schooling. You made money by inventing a gadget to sew clothes, is that it?'

'Yes. Well then, I asked myself what I could invent next. I came up with something which used the same idea, which is to say a needle going back and forth.'

The woman at Harker's side stopped speaking for a while, staring ahead at the bleak plain which they were traversing. Over to the left, they could hear the voices of Jemima and her son Pompey, as they talked over what had befallen each other since they had been separated a year or so earlier. It seemed to Harker that Abigail Tyler was choosing her words carefully. At last, she continued. 'Two things I hate. One's slavery and the other's war.'

Jed Harker said nothing, but sneaked a sideways glance at Abigail Tyler and said, 'So what did you come up with?'

'I asked myself what would happen if the bolt on a rifle, a repeating rifle you know, what if it went backwards and forwards rapidly, like the needle in a sewing machine. I figured that you could have a gun that fired more or less continual.'

'What would make it go back and forth?' asked Harker curiously. 'Meaning, what's powering it?'

'The recoil. As you fire, the recoil drives back the bolt and then a spring brings it forward again. An advantage would be that then you'd have a gun without hardly a bit of recoil.'

Harker pulled on the reins and halted the oxen. When the wagon had ground to a halt, he said, 'You tellin' me that you come up with this idea all by your own self?'

'Pretty much. There's others working on the same idea, but they're not doing so well. Man called Richard Gatling in New York and then over in Mobile, Alabama, there's a captain at the arsenal there called Gorgas, who's doing something much the same. I corresponded with them both, but they neither of 'em have anything like my device.'

'You're something else again, you know that?' said Harker, admiringly. 'I never heard the like. So where are you taking this little toy now?'

'You told me that you're not an abolitionist, Mr Harker.'

He said slowly, 'Well, I surely don't hold with buying and selling folk, like they was cattle, no. But then again, I ain't a great one for politics, neither.'

'There's no middle path. You're either for slavery or against it. One or the other, not both.'

Not wishing to debate the topic, for fear that

64

Abigail would prove the stronger protagonist in such a contest, Harker said, 'You've yet to come to the point, you know. Meaning, you haven't said how this invention of yours is going to have any bearing on anything.'

'Oh, but don't you see? Right now, all the slave states are about ready to boil over. Everywhere you go, all you hear is about states' rights and the rest of it. Give it a year and I'll take oath that at least a half dozen will have worked themselves up into a fit state to try and secede from the Union. Washington won't wear that and they'll come to blows.'

'I don't say you're wrong, but I can't see where this new gun of yours has any bearing on the case.'

Abigail Tyler didn't speak for a while. Jemima and her son were looking over towards the wagon, wondering perhaps what the delay was. The woman had her infant in her arms and put Harker strangely in mind of some of the chromo prints he had seen of religious subjects, such as the Madonna and child. He said, 'We can talk while we move, I guess,' and jerked the reins to get the oxen going again. 'I won't feel easy 'til we've put a fair bit of distance 'tween ourselves and that town.'

Jed Harker was feeling more and more uncomfortable about the fact that he and Miss Tyler were sitting up here at their ease, while the black folk were trudging along on foot. He said, 'Miss Tyler, I think we ought to let the others have a go of sitting, while we walk. It's only right.'

Abigail Tyler looked at him as though he had taken leave of his senses. She said, 'Why, my shoes aren't precisely suited to travelling 'cross rough ground like this. . . .' She stumbled to a halt, because she had suddenly realized that Jemima and her elder son were both barefoot. She said wonderingly, 'I swear to you, I never thought once of that. Meaning that that woman and child have no shoes at all on their feet. Isn't that strange?'

'My grandpapa, he had a saying. "Fine words butter no parsnips!" All well and good talking fancy about the rights of man and such, but when we've shoes on our feet and others are going unshod, well, something's amiss.' He called over to the others, crying, 'I wonder if the two o' you could favour us with a moment of your time. We've something to say.'

When Jemima and Pompey were walking along-side the wagon, Harker said, 'Time you two had a go at resting your legs, I reckon. Either of you ever drove oxen?'

'I can drive a team, sir.' said Jemima. 'Well as a man, I reckon.'

'Well then, you and your boys hop up here and me and this lady will go along by shank's pony for a spell.'

It was as he climbed down from the driving seat that Harker saw something which caused his heart to sink. They were working their way up a slope which led to the foothills of some mountains; which they were intending to skirt around, in order to enter the

Indian Nations from the east. This line of travel had meant that since leaving Abednego Jackson's home, they had been steadily rising and now they were at a height of perhaps 3-400 feet above both Jackson's house and also Lovett. A column of grey dust hung in the air and seemed to Harker's eyes to be moving more or less in their direction. He couldn't be sure at that distance, since he was unable to distinguish individual figures, but if he was any judge of the signs, this indicated a party of at least a dozen riders coming on towards them. They were probably at least five, maybe six miles away, but even at a trot they would be upon them within an hour.

'I don't like to alarm anybody,' said Harker casually, 'but given the signs over yonder, I'd say we're the object of some pursuit. It may be that those riders have no interest in us, but I wouldn't bet a dime on it.'

At his words, Jemima gave an unearthly shriek, redolent of fear and despair and she looked as though she were about to fall to the ground. Harker said, 'Hold up, ma'am. It ain't time to give up yet. Pompey, take that baby from your ma, or she's like to drop it.'

He looked around, to see if there was any hope of hiding. There was nothing, other than a pile of boulders a few yards from the trail. They might, at a pinch, be able to crouch behind them, but the wagon would betray their whereabouts at once. He said, 'Miss Tyler, less I'm mistook, you've got some sample of this wonderful new weapon o' yours in those crates. Am I right?'

'Yes, I have two of them.'

'You've ammunition for them too?'

'Yes, one of the boxes is full of cartridge.'

'Think you could instruct me in the use of the things inside a half hour?'

Abigail Tyler's face was drawn and white, but she replied quickly enough, saying, 'Yes, there's naught to the matter. I'll load them and you only need pull the trigger.'

Harker said, 'What it is, even if you and me hide behind those rocks and start firing our rifles at those men as they come on, they'll split up and take us anyway. If those guns of yours can lay down enough fire, we might just have a chance.'

If there was to be fighting, then Harker wanted all the party out of sight and under cover, so that he had a free hand with his shooting, without fretting about hitting those on his own side. He shepherded Jemima and her children behind the rocks and said, 'Don't be afeared, ma'am. I'll do all in my power to stop any harm befalling you and yours. Just keep your heads down is all.'

When he got back to the wagon, it was to find that Abigail Tyler was prising up the lids on two of the wooden boxes. Both looked to be full of straw, but when she delved inside, she hauled out a long black gun which looked like nothing Harker had ever seen before. For one thing, it was entirely made of gleaming, dark blue gunmetal. Even the stock looked to be made of metal, with no wood to be seen on it at all. The stock was a skeleton butt; no more than a triangular frame. Harker said, 'What rate of fire can you achieve with this thing?'

'About 300 shots a minute,' said the woman, as she reached into the other box and brought out a large, circular piece of metal which was about the size of a dinner plate.

'You can't be serious?'

'You think I'm apt to be joshing with you at a time like this?' As she spoke, Abigail Tyler was taking brass cartridges from the crate and fitting them into the metal disc. Now he could see more clearly, Harker saw it was really a thin drum. As she worked, the woman said, 'There's not much recoil. I've fired this and I hardly felt a thing. But keep your finger on the trigger and swing the gun slowly in an arc while it's firing.'

'Swing it in a what? An ark, did you say?'

'Just a narrow bit of a circle. I chopped a tree down using this thing, when I was testing it with that fellow who died yesterday.'

Glancing up, Jed Harker observed that the group of horsemen were a good deal closer now than they had been before. He could pick out individual riders now and they couldn't have been above three miles off. He counted eleven horses.

'You know,' said his companion in a conversational tone of voice, as though the information were of no great import, 'those men are as like to be after me and what's in this wagon as they are to be recovering any runaway slaves.'

'You think these are friends of that fellow I took out yesterday?'

'Truth to tell, I think there's a few men in the south who'd like to speak to me and see these weapons.'

The personal dispute between he and Chappe, combined with the little matter of aiding and abetting a black family escaping to the north, had rather driven all thoughts of the circumstances of his meeting Abigail Tyler the previous day out of his mind, but now Harker began to mull the question. He said, 'You're that important to them?'

'It's the difference between them having a racing chance for independence from Washington and knowing that they're like to be under the thumb of the Federal government forever.' She had finished charging or loading the black metal drum now and placed it on top of the strange looking rifle. It snapped home with a satisfying click. She handed the weapon to Harker, saying, 'Just recollect what I said, aim at the end man in the line and then keep firing while you move the sight across the whole boiling lot of 'em.'

Despite his extensive experience in warfare, Jed Harker had no desire at all to massacre a bunch of strangers and still hoped that it might be possible to parlay with the men coming on towards them; who were now only a mile or so off. These pacific inclinations were rudely dispelled when one of the men raised a rifle and sent a ball whistling in Harker's direction. Whether it was meant as a warning shot or a signal to surrender, he had no idea, but at that range whoever had fired on them was running the risk of causing injury or death. The ball went wide, but as far as Jed Harker was concerned, this act brought him personally into the quarrel. Any man who fired in his direction was declaring himself fair game for Harker's gun; that at least was the way that he saw the case. He said, 'Are those fellows only after what you got in those boxes or are they aiming to take you too?'

'I think that they want to take me alive, but that if I'm killed, that will satisfy them just as well. I have plans for my gun. Just with those alone, you could start production in a cannon factory.'

'Then I reckon we'd best hunker down behind this wagon of your'n and get ready to defend ourselves.'

Of all the reactions which Harker might have expected to this grim declaration, the one he received from the woman was the last he would have looked for. She threw back her head and laughed, saying, 'You got the case all wrong. It's them boys as will need to defend themselves against us!'

As though she had read his mind, the woman said, 'They aren't going to shoot up the wagon. There might be nitro in it and they don't want to destroy what's here. If they get close enough to be sure, they might try and take us, but they'd be fools to risk hitting these crates.' When Harker began to ask a question, touching upon his reservations about taking part in a battle while sitting next to a quantity of high explosives, Abigail Tyler interrupted him, saying, 'Look now, those boys are on the move.'

It was true; Harker looked to his left and confirmed that the riders were indeed on the move. They were strung out in a line and he could see that once they attacked at the gallop, then there was not the least chance that he and the woman – no matter how good shots they both might be – would be able to get every one of the men before they were upon them. The case looked utterly hopeless and Jed Harker wondered whatever could have possessed him to become embroiled in such a lost cause. He, who was always so careful of his own skin, found himself now allied with a complete stranger against insurmountable odds!

Instinct took over and Harker rested the strange-looking gun on the side of the wagon, with the muzzle pointing outwards at the advancing riders, who were now only a couple of hundred yards away and coming on at a trot which, if he was any judge of cavalry tactics, would soon be quickened to a canter and then a gallop. He sighted down the barrel and took aim at one of the men in the centre of the line. From what he could see, these men were all kitted out like irregular forces or bandits. They carried themselves like soldiers though and he wondered if they might be regular troops in civilian clothing.

The horsemen had reined in about fifty or sixty yards off and one of them called out, 'You folk lay down your weapons and I promise you'll come to no harm. You know what we want.'

At this moment, Jed Harker had a premonition, although as a plain, simple sort of fellow, he had no use generally for those who foresaw the future. He realized suddenly that whatever business these men had with Abigail Tyler and her boxes, he himself was surplus to requirements. They would be unlikely to leave a witness to what they were doing and the most likely outcome if he threw down his gun would be that they would shoot him out of hand. The boy and his mother would also end up back as slaves, most likely. It was this which decided him. He muttered, 'What the hell!' under his breath and pulled the trigger of the ungainly weapon which he was wielding.

Harker's first impression was of the terrific din which the weapon made; the explosive hammering sounded like an iron foundry at work. He was also aware that for all the size of the gun, Abigail had been quite correct; there was very little recoil. He'd braced the stock against his shoulder as he would any rifle, but there'd been little need. Then he recollected what he'd been told and, keeping the trigger depressed, he turned the gun through a narrow curve, trying to cover all the men. As he fired, the used brass cartridges flew out of the side of his weapon; ejected by some mechanism, presumably. Abruptly, silence fell. He was seemingly out of ammunition. Instinctively, he ducked his head down, fearful of the firing which must inevitably come in reply to his own shots. There was nothing. He peeped over the board and was astonished to see that all the men and half the horses appeared to be dead. The scene didn't make any sense to Harker. Surely, he alone could not have wrought such devastation with just this one weapon? The surviving horses wandered aimlessly about and even at that distance, he could hear the whinnying of the injured animals, mingling with the groans and cries of what he supposed must be wounded men.

Abigail Tyler was beside herself with glee, which Harker found distasteful. She cried, 'First field test! Just look what it achieved. Thought I was exaggerating or bluffing, did they? Well, sir, I guess they'll be obliged to own as they were wrong after this.'

'Hush up now,' said Harker, more than a little scandalized, 'it ain't fitting to carry on so when men have died. Show some respect.'

'Fiddle-de-dee, but you're a delicate one and no mistake. I didn't have you pegged for a man who'd behave so.'

'It's a fearful thing to kill a man, no matter if it's in battle or anywhere. Those men fired on me, which made this defence in a manner of speaking, but that don't mean I'm glorying in what I done.'

74

The woman had the grace to look a little sober at these words and said defensively, 'Well, they were dirty slavers, weren't they?'

'They were fellow beings,' said Harker, 'whatever else they mighta been.'

When they realized that the fighting was over and they weren't about to be dragged back into captivity, Jemima and Pompey came out from behind the rocks. Harker said, addressing his words to all of the others, 'Stay here a spell, while I go and see what's what.' He saw that Abigail Tyler was disposed to argue the point and he raised his hand, saying, 'No, I don't know if any of those men are just wounded. All of you wait here.'

Once he reached the site of what Harker could only, in his own mind at least, term a massacre, he found that one of the men he had shot was still alive. He went over to see what could be done. As he walked towards the wounded man, he kept a weather-eye out for any sign that the fellow might be about to gun him down, but he looked in too grave a condition for anything of the kind.

The first thing which Jed Harker observed when he came close to the injured rider was the terrible nature of his wounds. His right arm was all but severed, hanging off by a few shreds of muscle and he had a gaping hole in one of his legs. It looked to Harker as though death from blood loss could not be long delayed. He crouched down beside the man, who was probably younger than he himself, and said,

75

'Is there aught I can fetch, to ease you?'

'No, I'm shot to pieces,' came the reply, in a distinctive Virginia drawl. 'You took us all.'

'I'm sorry. It was you or me and I didn't want to die.'

'No, I see that,' said the dying man, a crooked smile on his lips. 'But it comes to us all. Have you a canteen? I'm powerful thirsty.'

By the time Harker had returned from one of the dead horses with a canteen, the man had died. Looking around at the bodies of horses and riders, he was amazed at the sheer amount of damage to flesh and blood that the gun he had used on them had caused. Instead of neat holes, the flesh of both riders and mounts was torn and shredded. The only injuries of this nature he'd seen in the past had been where artillery was used. Harker turned over all the bodies and examined them carefully. Then he went back to the wagon, where the others were waiting. He said, 'Miss Tyler, would you mind telling me one or two things about this business, such as how such harm has been caused. I seen a heap o' injuries from musket balls, but never the equal of this. It looks like these men were caught in a hail of canister-shot.'

'The ball is made special. Each has a gram of black Hercules decanted into it. You know what I talk of?'

'No, I haven't the least notion, but we'd best start movin' again and talk as we go. I think we arranged it so that you'd drive the oxen, ma'am,' Harker said, turning to Jemima. 'Pompey, you can help your ma, maybe hold the baby or something of the sort. Me and Miss Tyler have one or two things to discuss, so we'll walk a way off, if it'll cause no offence.'

Once they were on their way again, Harker remarked, 'What's this black something of which you spoke?'

'Black Hercules. It's nitroglycerine, but stabilized. You use black powder to soak it up, till it's a sticky liquid like porridge. The ball explodes when it hits something.'

'You dreamed this up?'

'Not the black Hercules, they use it for blasting on the railroads, but the idea o' putting it in the bullets is mine.'

CHAPTER 5

They continued in silence for a while. Jed Harker had a traditional view of womankind, which was that their natural sphere of activity lay in domesticity, rather than devising deadly weapons. There had been something cold-hearted about this woman's attitude to the death of a dozen men; the way that she talked of it as a 'field test'. While he was musing along these lines, the woman herself spoke, almost as though she'd been reading his mind.

'You think me an unnatural wretch, for not being grieved at the death of all those boys.'

'I wouldn't have put it so.'

'Whether or no, it's what you think. But I tell you, Mr Harker, there's a larger canvas here than the little corner that you can see. It's not a dozen men I'm thinking of or distressed over. It's the thousands or millions who are like to be saved by this gun.'

'I don't see that in any way at all,' said Harker in surprise. 'All I see is a quicker way of killing folk.

With a rifle, I might have killed three or four o' them boys, as 'tis, they're all of 'em dead. I don't see that as a way of saving life.'

Abigail Tyler said nothing, but looked annoyed. Harker continued, 'There's another matter I'd draw your attention to. My friend Chappe wasn't among those who lay dead back there, neither were those friends of his, Colonel whatshisname and the other. Which I take to mean that the party we lately crossed swords with were after you and not Pompey and his ma.'

'Meaning that we'll have another lot of enemies upon us in due season, is that how you read the case?'

'That's about the strength of it, yes.'

The track along which they were slowly moving ran between some low hills. To the right were higher hills and beyond them a range of mountains. The track they were on was not used over-much, for it led nowhere other than the Indian Territory and few people had business there.

The Indian Territory, known also as the Indian Nations, was land which had been ceded to the so-called 'five civilized tribes' in perpetuity, in return for their sacrifice of a vastly greater tract of land which the white men had required for their settlements and colonization. The five tribes comprised the Cherokee, Chickasaw, Choctaw, Creek and Seminole. They had been solemnly promised the land in which they now dwelt by the government in Washington and the treaties assured them that it would be theirs for all time. Already though, some in the government were repenting of this action, because the Indian Territory was of strategic importance, should the discontent in the South ever flare up into open rebellion. Theoretically, white men were forbidden from entering the district without the express permission of the chiefs of the five civilized tribes, but nobody worried over-much about such matters.

There was no clear border delineating the division of Arkansas from the Indian Nations and so Jed Harker and the others did not even notice when they moved from one area to the other. When the sun was at its highest point, Harker said, 'What do you say to stopping and eating for a short spell, Miss Tyler?'

'I say that's a right good idea. I'm famished.'

Jackson was seemingly no judge of how much three adults and a growing child would need to survive on for a few days. There was barely enough food for one picnic meal and the needs for provisions was like to become desperate by the next morning at earliest. They all sat in a little circle and ate some bread and cheese, washed down by draughts of water from a flagon which Abednego Jackson had also thoughtfully provided. As they ate, Harker did his best to set Jemima and her son at ease. He said, 'Have you lived long in Arkansas, ma'am?'

'I grew up on a plantation in the south,' she replied. 'Born and bred there.'

'You have any plans for when we get to the free states?'

'Mr Jackson, he done give me a letter for some folk who he say as'll help us.'

When he stopped talking, nobody else appeared to have any inclination to speak and so the meal proceeded in silence. After a while, Harker tried again. 'What about you, son? What's your tale?'

The boy cast a quick glance at his mother, as though to make sure that she had no objection to his speaking. Then, apparently satisfied, he said, 'They sell me off the plantation, 'way from my ma, almost a year back. That Frenchman, he buy me as a general servant.'

'What sort of master was he?' asked Harker curiously. 'I own I didn't take to him all that much.'

'He's a bad one,' said Pompey vehemently, 'as bad as can be. He hit me a whole heap.'

'Well, God willing, there'll be no more o' that. Once you're in Kansas, you'll be free as a bird.'

He had travelled a good deal in the course of his life, but Harker had never ventured into the Indian Nations. From what he heard, he had gathered it to be a lawless place; the haunt of fugitives and ne'er-do-wells. This was only hearsay and rumour though. He asked if any of the others had ever been through the territories or knew anything definite about it, but neither Jemima nor Abigail Tyler could tell him anything.

It didn't strike Jed Harker that it would be wise to

linger any longer, only a short ride from the scene of what could only be described as a massacre. For one thing, he had no idea if the men he had lately killed had been part of a larger group, but there was also the question of Chappe and his comrades. There was a personal grievance between him and Chappe and from what he had seen of the fellow, Harker had an idea that the swaggering little Creole would go to any lengths to avenge what he might see as a loss of face. Then too, he had Chappe's former slave with him and judging by the way that folk viewed things round here, Jed Harker's position would be seen less as a noble act in helping a poor soul to refuge, and more like the theft of a valuable horse or dog.

At Harker's suggestion, all four of them went on after the meal on foot, trudging along across the dusty and bleak landscape. He wished to let the oxen have as little work as could be for a while; they might have need of their stamina later and it wouldn't do to wear them out before it was seen what the future held.

They had seen nobody since the brief battle earlier that day; not so much as a single soul. This suited Harker well enough; he hoped to make it all the way to Kansas without encountering anybody, if it could be managed. Not that he expected this to be how things panned out. There was something about Abigail Tyler which seemed to invite trouble. Since first meeting her, it appeared to Harker that his life had been one round of shooting and death. He had met people like her before, although these had all been men. Such individuals attracted trouble, like shit draws flies. They were like lightning conductors, always with trouble crackling around them. Meeting a woman who drew violence and danger down like that was by way of being a novelty, but not in a pleasurable way.

For the rest of the afternoon, they walked along beside the ox-cart, letting the animals move at more or less their own pace. Every so often, the two beasts would grind to a halt entirely and then Jed Harker took the whip from where it lay on the buckboard and lashed them a few times, until they consented to start moving again. From time to time they halted for brief rests, but Harker was anxious to get as far as could be from the site of the recent killings of the southerners.

They camped that evening next to a little stream. The sun was fat and red on the western horizon and they were all bone-weary from having walked so long and far. Harker would by no means agree to their lighting a fire, as he had not the least desire to draw any kind of attention to their presence in this land. He said, 'We best sleep now and then rise and be on our way as early as can be tomorrow. Sooner the better. I want to strike camp 'fore dawn if we can.' So tired were the others that they seemed content to accept Harker's suggestion.

While he had been setting out his plans for their rest and so on, Harker had been eyeing Pompey and when the others had nodded their agreement to an early sleep, followed by an early rise the next day, he said to the boy, 'We need somebody to be awake and on guard. I'll take first watch and then wake you about two or three. That all right for you, son?'

Pompey glanced to his mother, who nodded her head.

'I reckon so, sir,' said Pompey, obviously proud to be considered enough of a man to keep watch over the camp at night.

During those long, lonely hours between dusk and the early hours of the morning, Jed Harker tried to cipher out to his own satisfaction how it was that he had become embroiled in such a snipe hunt as this. He was bound to admit that it was partly his own fault. He never had been able to turn a blind eye to the mistreatment of a child and it had also been a fundamental tenet, drummed into him by his father, when he was being raised, that a real man always goes to the aid of a woman and protects the helpless to the best of his ability. To that extent, helping the woman fix up her ox-cart and then interfering with the man striking the child were just what Harker did and always had been in the habit of doing. Never yet though had his natural tendency to care for the interests of the widow and orphan, as scripture put it, led him into such a curious position.

When he judged from the position of the stars wheeling overhead that it was about two in the morning, Harker woke Pompey by shaking his shoulder gently and said, 'Your turn to set watch.' Then he went off and lay down. He drifted off almost as soon as he closed his eyes and slept the sleep of the just until just after sunrise, when the little camp was overrun by a body of heavily armed men.

The first that Jed Harker knew of any trouble was when he was prodded roughly in the chest with the barrel of a Sharps carbine. His eyes snapped open and he saw immediately that young Pompey had been a most unreliable guard, for the boy lay snoring next to his mother, still unaware of what was happening. This, reflected Harker resignedly, was what tended to occur if you relied upon anybody but your own self!

There were about a dozen men milling around the place. They were Indians, but just precisely what tribe they might have belonged to, Harker had not the remotest idea. Most of them were wearing ordinary clothes, shirts and pants, rather than being dressed like traditional braves. To Harker's eye, they looked like a mighty experienced and disciplined bunch of men. All were carrying rifles and pistols and there was an air of quiet determination about them. What they wanted was anybody's guess and Harker's chief concern was that there were two fairly young women to be had there. If that was the way that these fellows' minds were tending, then all he could do would be to go down fighting in the defence of the women and child, although the eventual outcome of such a skirmish could be in no doubt. He was about to ask the men what they were after, when one of them, presumably the leader, forestalled him, by asking the self-same question of Harker. The tall, copper-coloured man, as lithe and muscular as a mountain cat, said, 'What are you doing in this land?'

Well, thought Harker, at least there wouldn't be any difficulties in communicating! He said, 'We're just passing through, nothing more than that.'

'Where? Are you going south or north?'

'Kansas.'

The warrior, for such he obviously was, cast his eyes around at Jemima, who had now awoken and Pompey, who had not. He said, 'Are these your slaves? You're a southron?'

'Not a bit of it. Meaning I ain't a southerner, nor these folk are my slaves. I'm helping them to get north, to be free.'

The man said nothing for a second or two, but looked at Jemima and her children. Pompey was still sound asleep and Harker thought wrathfully of what he would have to say to that young man, should they escape from this present predicament alive. The leader of the Indians addressed Jemima directly, saying, 'Is this the truth? Don't be afeared. You can talk honestly.'

Two things struck Jed Harker while all this was going on. The first was the beautifully correct and formal English that the leader of the Indians spoke. He wondered if he had learned to speak so in a mission school. The other, and more urgent consideration was where these men might stand as regarded the brewing trouble between the Yankees and the south. There were rumours that some in the south had promised the Indians that their territories would be able to apply for statehood in the future. This offer was meant to ensure that in the event of an armed struggle some time, which seemed increasingly likely, then the Indians would know which side to support. If these fellows were minded to believe such stories, then they might not take too kindly to seeing their territory used for conveying freed slaves to the north.

Jemima was voluble in her defence of Jed Harker and his intentions, telling the Indians that if it hadn't been for this kind gentleman, then she and her son would not have been reunited. During this explanation, Pompey woke up and at once glanced guiltily across to Harker. The boy clearly knew that it was his sleeping, when he should have been watching out, which had led to this present pass.

So far, Abigail Tyler, who was also awake now, had not spoken, but after Jemima had given her own account, she said to the man in whose hands their fate apparently rested, 'What are you going to do with us?'

While the man who seemed to be in charge was talking with them, the other Indians had stopped moving around and were seemingly waiting for instructions. They had not, Harker observed, taken anything and did not appear to be bent on looting or rapine. He formed the impression that they were genuinely curious about what he and the others were doing in their district, which was reasonable enough. It was a fair bet that if a bunch of Indians hunkered down for the night in an area of farmland, up in Wyoming say, then some of the locals would come and ask them what they were about.

After giving the matter some thought, the Indian said, 'I'm not going to do anything with you. If you women are being protected by this man, then you can carry on up to Kansas. But you ought to know that the storm is coming.' Miss Tyler and Jemima looked at the sky fearfully, as though fearing that they were about to be caught out of doors in a downpour, but Jed Harker chuckled.

'I apprehend your meaning,' said Harker. 'I'd say we're in for a real storm before too long. I'll make sure to get these folks under cover before it breaks.'

The tall, handsome young Indian nodded, satisfied that Harker had the message. Then he said, 'If you're wanting food and company, a man called Abbot runs an eating house and trading station, about twenty miles north of here.'

Then, without being given any orders, the whole party of Indians simply walked away. They had no mounts that Harker could see and neither then or later did he ever work out who they were and what they had been doing when they stumbled across him and the others. What was as plain as a pikestaff was that those men knew of some trouble brewing and it had been right kind of them to tip him the wink.

After the Indians had left, Harker gestured to Pompey and indicated that he wished to exchange a few words with the boy. The youngster approached him fearfully, fully aware that by slumbering when he should have been on watch, he had put them all in jeopardy. So dejected did the boy look, that Harker could not bear to scold him, especially since he had just that moment recalled an incident from his army days. He said, 'All's well that ends well, son. Mayhap if you'd warned me of those boys' approach, I might have reached for my gun and things could have ended worse than they did. There's no harm done.'

'You ain't angry with me, sir?'

'I'm not angry. I was recollecting a second ago 'bout a similar incident from my own life. I was a soldier you know, and setting on guard duty at night. Just like you. And like you, I drowsed off. My sergeant, he came across me while I was a slumbering and he struck me on the head with the butt of his musket. That woke me up sharp enough, I can tell you!'

'It won't happen again, sir. Swear to God.'

'I know it won't, don't fret about it.'

When Pompey walked away, Harker could see Jemima watching them anxiously, presumably afraid that he had been giving her son a tongue-lashing. He smiled reassuringly at her, but she cast down her eyes, as though unwilling to meet his gaze.

After breaking their fast as swiftly as could be, Harker harnessed up the wagon and they began on their way. He took the reins for the first part of the journey, for he wished to make sure that they made good speed during the morning and he was by no means convinced that either of the women could get as much lively action from the two oxen as he himself was able to manage. The less time that they spent in the territories, the better that he would like it. He just wanted to get to Kansas, see Jemima and her children handed over to a good person and then be free to continue with his own life.

Scattered throughout the Indian Territories were various establishments which catered for the needs of both the Indians and also any white men who happened to be around. Some were mission stations, others were trading posts, eating houses and saloons. In the main, they served just one section of the society; either Indians or white folk. The mission stations, for example, ran hospitals and schools for the indigenous inhabitants of the area and likewise the trading posts too were patronized almost exclusively by the red man. Those places traded pelts for cooking utensils and so on. The saloons, more like Mexican cantinas than any saloon such as you might encounter in more civilized parts, were for white men. It was, nominally at least, illegal to import intoxicating liquor into the Indian Nations, but nobody much minded the law and the border was too long and porous for there to be any hope of stamping out the trade in whiskey.

There were a few commercial undertakings which dealt with both the white man and the red; Joe Abbot's place was one such. Years ago, Abbot had built from stone a house and then erected at the rear, in a wooden, lean-to shanty, a little drinking den. He traded with the Indians, buying furs and even nuggets of gold in exchange for anything from whiskey and mirrors to modern rifles. He was a close trader and drove a hard bargain, but Abbot was a fair man and it was this which had prevented anybody murdering him and looting his stores. If not for men like Joe Abbot, then the supply of weapons and liquor into the Indian Nations would have long ago dried up. If murder and robbery became the order of the day, then this would hardly benefit anybody.

One circumstance of Joe Abbot's life which might be touched upon here, as it had some bearing on what later followed, is that he had a squaw-wife, who conducted the chief of his business with the Indians who wished to barter their goods. Like her husband, she drove a hard bargain, but never cheated or short-changed anyone. And if she favoured members of her own tribe, the Choctaws, nobody thought any the less of her.

Jemima was walking along, her baby in her arms, with Pompey at her side. Abigail Tyler strolled along, a little apart from them; evidently buried in her own thoughts. She glanced over in Harker's direction and seeing him looking towards her, smiled and came over to the wagon. Since the wagon was only proceeding at an easy walking pace, it was the work of a moment for her to swing herself up and then seat herself next to Harker. Once she was settled there, she said nothing for a minute or so and then abruptly observed, 'Somebody's sweet on you!'

At first, Jed Harker didn't take her meaning, but when he realized what she was hinting at, he found to his annoyance that he was flushing like a schoolgirl. He said gruffly, 'Don't be so foolish.'

'It's true,' said Abigail, 'Don't tell me you ain't noticed how she looks at you? Kind of like a puppy dog.'

Seriously annoyed now, Harker said stiffly, 'I'll thank you not to talk so, Miss Tyler. In the first place it's a heap o' foolishness and secondly, it ain't fitting.'

The woman shrugged pettishly and said, 'Well, you've only yourself to blame. I doubt any man's ever treated her so.'

'Why, what can you mean?' Harker asked in amazement. 'I treat her just exactly the same as I would any other woman who I didn't know well.'

'Yes, that's what I mean.'

Because this sounded so puzzling to Jed Harker and because the fact he was anxious not to have any ill-feeling while they were all travelling together, he thought it prudent to change the subject and said, 'I don't recall that you ever did tell me how this gun of yours is going to put an end to war. All I see is another way of killing men more quickly.'

Abigail Tyler still seemed, for reasons which he could not fathom out, a little vexed with him. At length, she said, 'Nobody can see it, not 'til I set the matter put plainly. All right, suppose you're fighting a man with your fists.'

'Then what? I can picture that easy enough.'

'You might carry on until one of you wins, is that right?'

'I guess,' said Harker, not seeing where this was leading, 'but what of that gun of yours?'

'Say you and a bunch of others were fighting and then a man showed up carrying a pistol and told you to stop doing it, what would you do?'

'You mean that me and the others only have our bare hands and this other fellow has a firearm? Why, I reckon as we'd mind him and do as we was bid.'

'Yes, that's what I thought you'd say.'

'Sorry, I still don't get it.'

There was a pause, while Abigail Tyler marshalled her thoughts. Then, she said, 'One man with one of my guns could hold off a whole regiment. Imagine if he was behind a barrier, or hiding in a hole. He'd only need to fire at the approaching men and they wouldn't be able to come nigh to him. Any army that had some of my weapons, there'd be no point anybody else fighting them. They'd lose. It would make war impossible.'

Harker, who had some experience of warfare, thought this over for a space and then remarked, 'Sounds like it could also make a bad leader all but invincible. I guess it depends who has these things.'

Abigail lowered her voice and said in a hushed tone, 'Well then, I've been told that Mr Lincoln himself wants to see my invention. I reckon as you couldn't say he's a bad man? If the Federal army has my guns, they'll be unbeatable anywhere.'

'You mean that this country would be able to rule the whole of North America? And further maybe?' Harker chuckled. 'What happens when some other boy gets hold of something of the kind? You ever think of that?'

'That man Gatling I told you about, he's top of the tree right now. His gun weighs a couple of hundred-weight and it's the size of an artillery piece. Needs a horse to tow it along with a limber and a crew of three to operate it. Nobody's got anything like my gun. The only plans in the world are right here with us.'

He shrugged. 'If you say so, Miss Tyler. All I say is, you ain't seen much o' the world.'

Irritated to find that her grand notions were being received in such a casual and almost dismissive fashion, Abigail Tyler changed the subject, saying, 'Is that house ahead of us, where we're heading for?'

A bulky, grey stone building could be glimpsed about a mile and a half along the track they were following. Smoke trickled up to the sky from a chimney and if he hadn't been told about it, Harker would have assumed the place to be a farmhouse. In fact, when Joe Abbot first settled in the Indian Nations, he had thought of farming, but found that the yearly cycle of agricultural enterprise, coupled with the unremitting uncertainty of profit, made this too chancy a prospect. Instead, he had settled firstly upon gun-running and moonshining and then, for the better part of the last ten years, upon running a cantina and trading post.

The business part of Abbot's establishment consisted of a wooden structure which leaned crazily against the side of his house. It could accommodate perhaps a dozen seated men at full capacity. Abbot had long ago given up trying to vary the fare which he offered. It was easier to dish out pork and beans to eat, with either whiskey or water to drink. The men who fetched up there were drifters and shady types who were on the scout. No questions were ever asked about a fellow's antecedents or plans. Abbot's place was simply somewhere to refuel, rest and perhaps pick up news about anything going on in the territories; posses, braves on the warpath and suchlike.

All Jed Harker had in mind when they drew up at Abbot's place that day was some hot food and perhaps buying some supplies; maybe bread, cheese and similar simple and wholesome comestibles. As soon as he and his party entered the lean-to though, he knew he'd taken a wrong turning. It was not that the hum of conversation died away and the half dozen men sitting there began staring at the intruders. That was only to be expected and in a similar position, he himself might have had his curiosity aroused by the sight of a white man in company with a mixed crew of black and white women and children. He would be the first to own that it must have looked a little strange. There was more to it than that though. There was an unmistakable and distinct air of hostility. Harker had encountered this far too often in the past to have any doubt about the matter. For reasons at which he could scarcely hazard a guess, the men seated at the rough, wooden benches were ill-disposed towards his presence there.

Had he been alone, Harker might well have been inclined to walk right back out of the little drinking den and try his luck elsewhere. As it was, he had two women, a child and a baby to watch over, as well as his own self, and so felt that he should try and tough it out. After all, they really were in need of some vittles. The food that they had might last today, but they'd be going hungry tomorrow unless they could lay hands on something more. So he shepherded his little band up to the plank laid across a couple of barrels which served as a counter and asked Joe Abbot what there was to eat.

Abbot, who was supremely indifferent to anything beyond strictly mercantile transactions, said, 'There's pork. Beans. Bread too, if you want it.'

Jed Harker turned to Abigail and Jemima, saying, 'Does that suit?'

'It's all one if it don't,' said Abbot, ' 'cause that's what there is.'

Jemima was looking around uneasily. She too had picked up a sense that they were not welcome. She said hastily, 'Just anythin'll be fine, sir.'

'What about you, son?' Harker asked Pompey. 'Pork and beans be good for you too?'

The boy nodded shyly and Harker said to Abbot, 'Well, I reckon that will be four helpings of your pork and beans then, if you please.'

It was at that moment that Harker felt a bony finger jab him in the back. He turned to face a mean-looking and weasel-faced runt of a man, who had come up behind him and was just standing there, staring menacingly at him. Harker said, 'Something on your mind, friend? Only don't go prodding me so. I don't take to it.' He spoke pleasantly, but his heart was troubled. Left to himself, he would be happy enough to set to with this fellow, but he had a greater responsibility towards the helpless folk in his care. He didn't think it would be right to cast himself into hazard, not unless it was quite unavoidable.

'What d'ye mean by it?' enquired the man pugnaciously. 'It's an insult to every man here.'

Genuinely foxed by what the fellow was driving at, Harker said in some bewilderment, 'You're insulted by me ordering pork and beans? Why, there's three men sat over yonder eating the self-same thing. What ails you?'

'You think this is funny?'

'Not a bit of it. What's your complaint?' Although he did not wish for trouble, Jed Harker's own fuse was none too long and if this fellow was really spoiling for a rough-house, then perhaps it would be as well to oblige him and have the matter out of the way.

'Bringing them,' the man indicated to Jemima and her children, 'in here. I ain't about to set next to a black while I'm eating.'

It really was on the tip of Harker's tongue to suggest that if he didn't find the company to his liking, then the man could take himself off to eat outside, but he restrained himself and said instead to Joe Abbot, 'You've no objection to my friends and I eating here?'

Abbot, married to an Indian himself, had no use for such foolishness and said loudly, 'I couldn't give a damn about the colour of a man or woman's skin. You got the money for food, you can set and eat it here, peaceable like.'

Harker escorted the two women to a bench, whereupon the two men sitting nearby, ostentatiously got up and moved to the other side of the room. The whole thing was so childish, that Jed Harker felt like laughing out loud. Instead, he settled the women and Pompey and then went up and paid Abbot for the food and took it over to the table. As he did so, Abbot said very softly, without looking at him, 'Have a care when you leave. Those boys'll dare do nothing here, but they might outside.'

Harker nodded imperceptibly to show that he had heard.

CHAPTER 6

The meal was filling and satisfying. Under more relaxed circumstances, Jed Harker would have lit his pipe and relaxed a little while his food digested. He felt instinctively though that this was not the smart dodge here and the sooner they made tracks, the better for all concerned.

Abbot was quite agreeable to selling them a loaf of bread, but had not enough supplies to go beyond that. The loaf they bought might be enough for one person for a day, but would hardly satisfy the four of them. Once this transaction had been completed, they left, with a view to continuing north. Harker was not overly surprised when he found the man who had challenged him for bringing black folk into the cantina, hanging around near the wagon. His heart sank and he decided that if needful, he would abase himself to this loathsome individual, if it meant avoiding trouble. It was plain from the start though, that this tack would not answer.

'You an' me got a crow to pluck,' said the man and Harker marked something he had not noticed earlier, that this fellow spoke with a distinct Virginia drawl. He seemed fated of late to be forever getting crosswise to southerners. Nevertheless, he did not despair of smoothing over this present unpleasantness.

'I'm a stranger in these parts,' said Harker, 'and if I upset some custom or other, I'm sorry for it. I hope we can part on good terms.' He extended his hand, hoping that the other would grasp it and accept his apology; whereupon the man from Virginia hawked and spat on the outstretched hand.

Now it was one thing to swallow pride when something greater than his own dignity was at stake, but quite another to allow a man to treat him in so disgusting a way. Jed Harker bent to the ground and wiped his hand in the dust to remove the saliva. While he did so, he never once took his eyes from the man who had spat on him. After rubbing the spittle from his hand, Harker stood up and said to Abigail and Jemima, 'You two stay here with the children. I needs must have a word or two with this fellow. It won't take above a few minutes.'

'A few minutes?' said the southerner, mockingly. 'A few minutes and you'll be lucky if your jaw ain't broke to atoms.'

Ignoring the other man, Harker handed his pistol to Abigail Tyler, saying, 'Keep ahold of this, if you will, Miss Tyler.' Then he undid his shirt and removed it, so that he stood stripped to the waist. He turned to the man who had spat on his hand and said, 'You want we should walk over there, out of the way a little, so that I might show you what I think of you?'

'You're damned right I will.'

'Watch your language,' said Harker reprovingly. 'Recollect that there are ladies present.'

The other men who had been eating and drinking in Abbot's place had by now wandered out to see the fun. Most probably, the man who had challenged Harker to a fight had announced his intention before getting up and coming outside. Harker had the feeling that popular opinion tended to be with his opponent and that those present would be pleased to see him cast down into the dirt. Whether or no, he was not about to let any living man treat him in that way and although it interfered somewhat with his desire to move swiftly north, he thought that it would be worth delaying by a few minutes in order to teach a man how to comport himself in a civilized manner.

Near to the house were two corrals, where the horses of those who stopped at Abbot's to either eat or trade were kept. A couple of the men who looked pleased at the diversion which a fist-fight might provide, jumped into one of the enclosures and shooed all the horses into the other. This left a large space, surrounded by post and rail, free for the contest.

101

Although he was a good fighter and pretty confident of coming out on top in a fair fight, Jed Harker was far from looking forward to fighting. For one thing, he didn't altogether trust the other men who were now clustering around the corral. If he beat their friend, would others then fall upon him like a pack of wild animals to revenge themselves upon Harker for both bringing a black person into the cantina and also defeating a comrade of theirs? As he neared the corral, he cast his eyes over the men standing around and noted that they did not look to him like roughnecks out on the scout. In fact, now that he was able to look at them more closely, he had again that strange feeling that he had had when facing the riders pursuing Abigail Tyler. It seemed to Harker that these men put him strongly in mind of regular soldiers dressed in civilian clothing. They carried themselves not in a slouching and undisciplined way, but rather as though they were used to standing up smartly and moving to order.

As Harker reached the corral, a man standing by the gate bowed mockingly and opened it for him. The man he was to face had already entered the corral by vaulting the fence; perhaps as a demonstration of his agility and physical prowess. One of those present took it upon himself to assume the role of Master of Ceremonies, announcing loudly, 'Gentlemen, there will be no kicking, biting, scratching or any other such underhand methods used. A good clean fight is what we're after.' Another southerner, judging by his accent, thought Harker. What was it with all the Georgians and Virginians he had encountered in the last few days? But there was no time to consider the question further, because his opponent, also stripped to the waist, was approaching him in a martial and aggressive way.

Ordinary fights between two men are frequently brief affairs. A few punches are thrown, a man falls to the ground and victory is declared. This is particularly so since the greater number of such events are fuelled by liquor. There is a flaring of anger, which soon subsides. Like as not, the late enemies will be found a half hour later drinking together as though naught has happened. Sometimes though, there is real hatred and contempt involved and then the struggle for mastery is apt to be prolonged; especially, as in the present case, when both men chanced to be young and tough.

Jed Harker was still unsure how things had come to this pass, but was quite determined that he was not going to be bested by this wretch. At first, the two of them circled warily around each other, as though they were dancing. Then the southerner darted in and landed a blow on the side of Harker's head, immediately retreating again. Then, as though by agreement, they closed in for battle, striking each other about the body and face, as and when they were able to get through the defences of the other. This went on for three or four minutes, it being pretty plain that the two men were evenly matched in strength and ferocity. The end of the fight came with shocking suddenness.

Possibly because he had hoped to achieve a more swift and decisive victory over Harker or perhaps due to some viciousness of character, the southron evidently had had enough of slugging it out. Maybe he thought that the longer the fight continued, the more he was revealed as a man unable to deliver a sharp lesson to somebody who had offended against sensibilities regarding the presence of black folk in a room where he was eating and drinking. Whatever the reason, he unexpectedly swung his booted foot at Harker's groin. Had the kick made contact, it would without the shadow of a doubt have ended the fight with Harker's defeat, but Jed Harker had seen enough dirty fighting for this gambit not to take him wholly by surprise. He succeeded not only in deflecting the foot, but also grabbing hold of the ankle and forcing the man's leg so high in the air that he overbalanced and toppled to the ground. In an instant, Harker was upon him; pinning him to the ground with his own foot planted firmly and immovably on the fellow's throat.

'That was a scurvy trick,' said Jed Harker, 'but no more than I would have expected from a filthy devil like you.' He paused and then asked courteously, 'I'm sorry, did you make some remark? I can't hear you!' This last was meant humorously, for the man upon whose neck he was standing was choking for breath and in no fit state to speak a word. Harker concluded by saying, 'Me and my friends is leaving now, and you'd be well advised not to follow us, for I tell you now that if I catch sight of you again after we leave, then I'm apt to shoot you down like the mangy dog you are.'

By the time that Jed Harker consented to raise his foot off the throat of his one-time adversary, the man's face was purple and he was gasping for air like somebody who has been almost drowned. It seemed to Harker that he had delivered a sufficiently stern warning and so he turned his back contemptuously on the fellow and began walking back to where Abigail Tyler and the others were watching. Despite his telling them to go to the wagon, they had all apparently been unable to resist the spectacle of a fight. Or perhaps it was that they all felt that they had a personal interest in the outcome of the contest since their own fortunes were now inextricably bound up with his own. Before he reached them, Pompey yelled urgently, 'Jed, behind you!'

That the boy had used Harker's given name was such a novelty that Harker knew at once that something was seriously amiss. He turned and saw that the man he had lately beaten was advancing on him with a knife in his hand. At a guess, he had had this hidden in one of his boots. Harker raised his hands, with the palms outwards, to indicate both that he had no weapon and that he meant no harm. He said, 'Ah, fella, you wouldn't go after an unarmed man with a knife, surely?' It was a meaningless delaying tactic,

105

until he could come up with some way of tackling the situation, but the other man did not so much as break step. It was tolerably plain to Jed Harker that this was likely to end in his murder, unless somebody intervened, and that right quickly.

The boom of the scattergun came as a shock to Harker and caused the man who was obviously intent upon killing him to stop dead in his tracks. They both turned to look at where the shot had come from and were in time to see Joe Abbot, who had just discharged his weapon into the air, lower it and point it in their general direction. He said, 'You there, with the knife in your hand. Just you drop it directly. And you, with your womenfolk and young 'uns, you take yourself away off out of it, before you cause any more of a disturbance. And don't neither of you think as I wouldn't shoot, because I tell you straight, I taken first pull on the trigger. Do as I say, the pair of you, or 'fore God, somebody's like to die.'

Nobody who heard Abbot speaking, doubted that he meant what he said. He gave every impression of a man who was mightily ticked off and really did not care for folk fighting and trying to kill each other in the vicinity of his home. When he thought that matter over later, Harker at first wondered if Abbot had come to his rescue out of a feeling of justice and motivated by a desire to save his life. After due consideration, he concluded that this was not at all the case and that the man had simply not wished to see any corpses lying around near his business, with the inevitable questions which might arise as a result. Nor did he want to see violent affrays, which could easily escalate into gunplay, being played out so close to his family home.

The man who, a moment earlier, had been aiming to knife Harker, opened his hand and let the blade fall to the ground. As soon as he saw this, Jed Harker said to Abigail and Jemima, 'Just get moving right now. I'll get the oxen going and the rest of you make haste.' It took only a minute to start the wagon rolling and then they were heading north again.

Why the man who had wished him harm did not simply wait a little and then saddle up with his friends and come in pursuit of him, to settle things away from Abbot's place, was something that Harker never figured out. Even after the wagon had been lumbering on for an hour, it would have taken a galloping horse only five or ten minutes to catch up with it. Still, there it was. He kept the carbine ready by his side and constantly craned his head round to check for any riders coming up behind them but there was nothing.

'That was exciting,' said Abigail Tyler, as she walked alongside the wagon. 'If that fellow hadn't fired off his shotgun, I don't know what would have happened.'

'I dare say I'd be no longer in the land of the living,' replied Harker. 'It's a very odd thing, Miss Tyler, but since meeting you, every man I encounter seems to be hell-bent on making an end to my life.'

107

She shot him a sideways glance, unsure whether or not he was speaking in earnest, before saying, 'I didn't have you pegged for the nervous type. I thought you had more grit.'

In spite of himself, Jed Harker chuckled at that. He said, 'You have a rare cheek, you know that? I never said I was nervous about folk trying to take my life. It's happened before and like as not will again. But this is the first time I've known men try to kill me once or twice a day.'

'How long before we reach Kansas, would you say?'

'We can count on another two nights in the territories, I reckon.'

As he chatted inconsequentially with Abigail Tyler, it occurred to Harker that he had been a little remiss in handing out thanks where it was due. He called over to Pompey, who was walking alongside his mother. 'Come over here a minute, would you, son? I got something to say.'

The boy looked a little uneasy at being called over in this way. It seemed to Harker that he might still be feeling a little guilty about sleeping when he was supposed to have been on sentry-go. To put the lad's mind at rest, Harker smiled broadly and, as he drew near, said, 'I owe you a debt of gratitude and I ain't afraid to own it. Had you not shouted out your warning, that villain might have caught me unawares.'

'It was nothin', sir. You woulda done the same for me.'

Harker smiled and said, 'You called me Jed then, time to drop all this sir once for all. What do you say?'

'All right . . . Jed.'

'That's the boy. I've a mind to have a few words with your ma. Think you could keep these beasts moving for a spell?'

'I'll surely try.'

'Then jump up here and take the whip. Make sure they don't forget who's in charge, there's no more to it than that.'

After he had jumped down from the buckboard, Harker went over to Pompey's mother. He reached out his hands and said, 'Why not let me carry the young 'un for a space, ma'am? You could do with a rest, I reckon.'

The woman gave him an odd look, but suffered him to take the baby. For a minute or two, they walked along in companionable silence. Out of the corner of his eye, Harker saw Abigail Tyler watching curiously, probably wondering what he wished to say to Jemima. Well then, let her wonder!

'It's no affair of mine,' said Harker, 'but I was thinking about what you and your children will be doing when you get to Kansas. Do you have a definite place where you'll be helped?'

The woman thought this over for a while before replying. Harker had the impression that she wasn't at all sure of his purposes and really, there was no earthly reason why she should trust him. She had certainly been ill-used enough, with her child snatched away from her. In her position, he too would be cautious about those around him. At length, she said, 'I been given the name of a church.'

'That all? You don't know the name of anybody at the church?'

'No, suh. Just the church name.'

'You ever been to Kansas?'

'Not nohow.'

Harker thought this over and then said, 'I'm not one to push in where I ain't wanted, but I don't feel easy in my mind about this. If you've no objection, I can stay with you until I see you safe in another's hands.'

Jemima turned her head and stared hard at Harker. They continued to walk side by side, with her scrutinizing him hard. He said, 'If I overstepped what's polite, I'm sorry. Forget I said anything.'

'Why'd you care what happens to me and mine?'

'What's right is right. You been ill-treated and you've nobody to look out for you. I'll take your part and help you if you'll allow me.'

'There's riders ahead. Whole heap o' them, judging by the dust they kickin' up.'

So engrossed had he been in the conversation, that Jed Harker had been focusing upon that to the exclusion of all else. Jemima was perfectly correct. On the horizon was a grey column which might at first sight be mistaken for a plume of smoke. It was though, as Jemima said, a cloud of dust kicked up by a troop of horses. As he watched, it did not appear to

110

Harker that the cloud was moving across his line of sight, which meant that the men producing it were not travelling at right angles to him. The inescapable conclusion was that those stirring up all that dust were heading either away from him or heading directly towards him. Since they had not been over-taken by anybody since leaving Abbot's place, it was a fair guess that these riders were not heading away from them.

Harker and the others were travelling across a featureless plain of scrubby grass, with little cover. Here and there were clumps of spindly trees and in the distance were low hills, but whatever they did, the wagon was likely to be seen by the men now approaching. Jed Harker could not think who these people might be; Indians seemed the most likely bet. They had been right lucky that morning with the ones that they had encountered, yet there was no reason at all to suppose that their good fortune would hold. Harker strode over to the wagon and told Pompey to rein in the oxen. If flight was impossible, then they would have to make their stand here. He said to Abigail, 'I'm half minded to break out one of those guns of yours. Only thing is, we've no idea how many men there might be, nor what they purpose. I wouldn't wish to start shooting if those men are just travelling through the territories like us.'

'You want I should prepare one of 'em, just in case?'

'No, I wouldn't say so,' said Harker slowly and thoughtfully. 'I've a notion that we might be making a rod for our own backs. Looking at that dust, I'm thinking that there's at least fifty horses, maybe more. I don't want to try conclusions with half a company, it would be madness. We'll have to bide here and see what chances.'

The closer that the riders came, the more Harker gained the impression of a tightly packed formation rather than a straggling band. This argued against Indians and in favour of some organized enterprise. What it might be, he had no idea and it wasn't until the oncoming body of men were just two or three miles off from them that Jed Harker realized what was to do. When it dawned on him, he gave a whoop of delight, like an excited child. The others looked at him nervously, as though he had taken leave of his senses. He turned to them and said, 'Why, lookee there! See who we've to deal with?'

'Who is it?' asked Abigail Tyler in some perplexity.

'You can't see the blue coats? Those are US cavalry or I'm a Dutchman. This is a turn-up for the book and no mistake.'

Now they knew what they were supposed to be looking for, the others strained their eyes to see if Harker was right. Squinting across the intervening miles, both women could now see that there was indeed a tingle of dark blue, visible through the haze of dust which was being kicked up by the horses.

'I'll be damned,' said Abigail, oblivious to the

looks which both Jemima and Harker gave her at such profanity. 'It's true. I reckon this is a sight for sore eyes. With luck, I can deal with those boys.'

It took a good thirty or forty minutes for the troop of cavalry to reach them. There were, as Harker had already calculated, more than fifty riders and they were proceeding in military formation as though alert for trouble. As the main body drew nigh, Harker saw that there were flankers out about a mile to either side of the column. He figured that there was some trouble with the Indians and was mightily relieved to find that the army was now at hand. He marked that there were no supply wagons or auxiliaries and this struck him as a little odd. These men gave every appearance of being ready to give battle at the drop of the proverbial hat.

The officer leading the column called a halt when he came to the wagon, with its little cluster of people. He said to Harker, 'What the devil are you civilians doing here?'

'Civilians?' asked Harker, a little nettled. 'Wasn't aware that there's any particular reason why we shouldn't be here. This isn't a battlefield nor anything of the sort, I reckon.'

Abigail Tyler, irritated at Harker's tone of voice, interrupted at this point and said, 'You must forgive my friend. We really are very glad to see you. I'm heading north with something of great importance for your army. I have a letter from an official in Washington, if you'll give me a moment to fetch it from my bag.'

'Begging your pardon, ma'am, but we all seem to be talking at cross-purposes here. Happen I should set things straight.' Turning to Harker, he continued, 'As for my talking of civilians, the reason is that this area is now under martial law. I have authority to do pretty much as I wish and one of the things I wish is to have no civilians sassing me or questioning my authority.'

This was a facer and Jed Harker hardly knew how to respond. He said wonderingly, 'Martial law? What's going on, Major?'

Slightly mollified at being addressed by his correct rank, the officer said, 'The order declaring martial law was only issued yesterday and it's not in reason that you should have heard of it. I'm guessing that you folk are refugeeing north. Meaning, you ain't southerners?'

'Not a bit of it,' replied Harker. 'We hope to reach Kansas either tomorrow or the day after.'

'You stick to that plan and you might do well enough. You ask what's going on. There's a war coming, that's what. Mr Lincoln has called for volunteers and we've been sent to secure this corner of the territories against invasion.'

Harker felt dizzy; he had not the faintest idea of what was happening. He said, 'I'm a little behind the times, it seems. Who's the enemy?'

The major looked at Harker in amazement and said, 'You've not heard about the shelling of the fort in Carolina? It was as good as a declaration of war.

114

The south is trying to break free of the union and we're the boys to put a stop to such games.'

Abigail Tyler exclaimed in the greatest excitement, 'You must help me to get north! I have something which will win this war. It's vital I get to the nearest town with a telegraph.'

'I don't know aught of that, ma'am,' said the major courteously. 'I only know what my orders are, which is to secure the southern part of this territory against any incursions.' There was nothing more to be said and after saluting her respectfully, the officer ordered his column onwards, in the opposite direction to that in which Harker, Abigail and the others were travelling.

After the cavalry had departed, leaving Abigail Tyler looking crestfallen, Harker said, 'We need to think now on what will be best.'

'What do you mean,' said Abigail, '"what will be best?" I thought we'd agreed that we were going to race to the border as fast as we can make it. We surely don't want to linger in the territories, especially now that we know that war is about to start.'

'That fellow, the major, he hasn't thought this through clearly,' said Jed Harker patiently. 'All he can think of is bugles and glory.'

'I suppose you know better than a professional soldier what's needful,' replied Abigail scornfully. 'I don't think it for a moment.'

Jemima and her son were watching Harker carefully. It was plain that they felt differently about the case and would be likely to follow his guidance. Perhaps this irritated Abigail Tyler, for she thought herself the equal of any man when it came to doling out helpful and useful advice. She said tartly, 'I'd have you recall that this is my wagon and my oxen. We'll go where I say and when I want.'

None of this seemed to affect Harker over-much, he merely remarked mildly, 'All I said was we need to think on it, nothing more.'

'Well then, what are your thoughts? Let's be hearing them!'

There was a pause, while Harker marshalled his ideas and set them out in the order that he wished to say them out loud. He had no doubt that he was in the right and that they were all in danger, but wished to put the case as fairly as was able.

At length, he said, 'Those horse-soldiers as just left us, they're looking for a clean fight against another band of cavalry. Swordplay and bravado and I don't know what all else kind of foolishness. There won't be nothing o' the sort. I been a soldier, I know about war and fighting. They ain't goin' to find a troop of horses blocking their path. Those boys we been coming across then and when, they don't even look like soldiers. They're not wearing uniforms or nothing. This is going to be a guerrilla war.'

'A what war?' asked Abigail. 'I don't follow you at all. Speak plainer.'

'Guerrillas is what you get sometimes, when a small bunch of men wish to harry a larger and better

116

armed group. They snipe, they raid, they come at night and cut throats. All that sort of trick. What you sometimes call irregular forces.'

'You think those southerners that have crossed our path are like that?'

'I'm altogether sure of it.'

For the first time, Jemima joined in the conversation, saying, 'What do you say we should do, sir?'

'That's what I been thinking about. Those boys'll not want open fighting with the US cavalry, but at the same time, they're goin' to want to secure this here part of the Indian Nations for their own purposes. If the major is right and fighting has begun, then this little area is going to be mighty handy for the side which holds it. Fact is, if we ain't careful, we're like to be caught between two fires. Three, even,' said Harker, rubbing his chin thoughtfully as he sought to order and arrange his thoughts.

'What d'you mean?' asked Pompey. 'If we've them union soldiers 'tween us and the southerners, don't that mean as we're safe now?'

Jed Harker smiled at the boy. He appreciated a sharp mind and it struck him that this lad had quicker wits than most boys of his age. He said, 'Well now, if we was talking of a regular battlefield, son, then you'd be about right. But we ain't. Fact is, this is about as far from regular warfare as you're like to see. Those southrons won't be wanting to meet a troop of cavalry head on. No, they'll seek to dodge round them, what we used to call outflanking, when

117

I was a soldier.'

'You really was a soldier, sir, I mean Jed?' asked the boy.

'That I was, but this ain't the time for reminiscing. It's enough that those boys, as I've already had the odd run-in with, will be racing along, trying to get to the border with Kansas and stake their own claim to territory. If what the major said is correct and the war's started, then I guess that there'll be reinforcements coming along to back up those guerrillas. Then it'll be that troop of men we saw who'll have to fight for their lives, on account of they'll be cut off behind enemy lines.'

The two women and the boy stared at Harker, plainly waiting for him to come up with a plan to save them. He found this a little irksome, for he liked to rely only upon himself and to be responsible for his own self. Then again, he could hardly abandon two women and two children to the vagaries of war. He said at length, 'Miss Tyler, I reckon that now would be a good time for us to break out that weapon o' your'n and load it up. Happen I'm wrong, and nobody would be more pleased about it than me, were it to prove so, but I guess that we've fighting ahead of us. We're apt to need any edge we can get and that gun is the hell of an edge, begging your pardon, ladies, for the language.'

'I see the two fires,' said Abigail Tyler, 'what's the third?'

'Why, the folk whose land we're in, of course,'

replied Harker in surprise. 'Do you think that they'll take kindly to a heap o' white men charging into their country and shooting each other up? According to the treaty, this here is almost on a par to being a sovereign nation. Can't see them not joining in, on their own account, if there's any fighting starts. Sooner we get out of this place, the better.'

In later years, it was said that the Indian Nations had supported the Confederacy and therefore forfeited their right to a country of their own, when once the War Between the States had drawn to a close. It wasn't really so; merely an excuse to allow the White Man to renege on his word and seize the territory of the Indian Nations, adding it to the state of Oklahoma. In truth, the Indians wished only to be left alone and had not the slightest desire to become embroiled in a squabble between and betwixt two sets of white soldiers. For now, the situation in which the little band found itself was far from enviable; caught between two bodies of armed men, with only one grown man to tend to their interests.

CHAPTER 7

What Jed Harker advised was that they headed off the track they were on and turned a little to the east. This would take them into a range of low hills, where they might not be so prominently exposed as was the case on the plain across which they were currently making their way. Abigail Tyler, for all her show of being well able to take care of herself, was secretly pleased that Harker seemed to know what he was about and was content to allow him to direct their course; at least for the time being. So it was, that within an hour of parting company with the cavalry, the ox-cart and the little body of people accompanying it were out of sight of the track and making their way across the coarse, sparse grass which covered the hills. It was easy enough to wend their way along the broad, shallow valleys which separated the hills. It would have been pointless trying to traverse a straight line, over the hills and then down to the valleys; to say nothing of such a course of action being likely to see them silhouetted periodically on the sky-line. Harker's chief aim at the moment was to pass as quietly through the Indian Nations as could be, without drawing any attention to themselves.

Pompey had taken to clinging to Jed Harker's side like a cockleburr. The news that Harker had been a soldier had cemented the esteem in which he held Harker and unless his mother called him away and told him not to bother the man, it seemed that all young Pompey wished to do was march along as close as could be to the man who had now evidently become some kind of hero in his eyes. Noticing this, Abigail waited until Pompey's mother had called him away on some errand and then hauled herself up onto the wagon and seated herself next to Harker, who was trying to get a little more speed out of the two sullen beasts who were hauling the cart along. She said, 'Well, looks like you got two admirers now. First the mother and now the son. Why, you've a ready-made family there, if only you were wanting to settle down when we get to Kansas.'

Harker shot her a disapproving look and said, 'The boy, he's of an age when he needs a man to look up to. I ain't what you'd call the right pattern, but we'll have to hope that Miss Jemima there, she picks up with somebody suitable.'

'You're as delicate as a woman with the way you talk and all. Anybody ever tell you so?'

'No,' said Harker equably, 'I don't recollect that anybody did.'

'You're that sensitive about being polite and doing the right thing and such.'

'Is that a bad thing?'

'No, just uncommon in a man, is all.'

Before heading off the track, Harker and Abigail Tyler had broken out one of her guns and loaded the drum which fed the ammunition to the breech fully with cartridges. Harker felt a little uneasy about leaving such a fearsome weapon untended in the wagon, but short of riding along with the thing cradled in his arms, he didn't very well see that he had another choice.

Every so often, Harker would invite Jemima and her son to take his place and steer the wagon. For all that he was bothered, he would have been quite content to let them sit up there, perched on the buckboard the whole time while he strode along at his own pace. The problem was that the two of them were nowhere near as adept as him at keeping the oxen moving and as soon as he got down, the lazy creatures seemed to sense that they could slow down to an absolute crawl and that they had nothing to fear from the whip.

At about midday, Harker began to think about what they would do for vittles that day. There was the loaf of bread that Abbot had sold them and other than that, just water. There was no shortage of water, because every so often they came across little rivulets and streams which crisscrossed the area they were travelling, draining rain from the surrounding hills.

He and Abigail Tyler were walking along now, leaving the wagon to the others. Harker said, 'Well, I reckon as I ought to think about providing some food, otherwise we're like to starve, never mind getting shot in a war or scalped by Indians.'

'What'll you do?'

'Shoot something, I reckon, though I've no idea what. Jack rabbit, maybe'

After instructing Jemima and Pompey to keep the ox-cart rumbling on as best they could, Harker slung the carbine which he had borrowed from Abigail Tyler over his shoulder and set off at a loping run to the crest of the nearest hill. He'd little apprehension of being left behind, not at the pace that the mother and son were managing to keep those oxen moving.

At a pinch, Harker was thinking that he might be able to bring down a bird, although he'd rather a scattergun than a military rifle for such a purpose, but what he really wanted was a buck or a rabbit or something which he could be tolerably sure of hitting with a single ball.

As he drew out of earshot of the wagon – and would in the normal way of things have expected to hear nothing other than the rustling of the wind in the grass and occasional birdsong – Harker gradually became aware of a background of sound; one which set his nerves taut and made him wonder if the best course of action might not be for him to race straight back to the others. At first, he couldn't rightly make out what he was listening to, other than that it evoked buried memories and made him alert for danger. It was nothing much, really. The creak of a harness, little grunts from men and whinnies from horses. The noise all seemed to be coming from beyond a hill away over to his right. This was crowned with a spinney of stunted trees, which had not yet any leaves on them. They would provide a little cover though, were he to creep up and have a peep over the brow of the hill and see what was what. He accordingly walked up the little rise aways and then crawled to the top; so as not to make himself prominent against the sky for anybody in the valley below. It was only just as he reached the clump of trees that he suddenly recollected what the sounds which he heard put him in mind of; an army camp being established in debatable territory, with minimum noise and fuss. It came therefore as no surprise when Harker finally peered over the crest of the high ground and spied fifty men or more, setting up tents and hauling three field guns into position.

At first, Jed Harker thought that he might be watching another detachment of Federal forces setting up a base, but that was before he noticed something exceedingly curious. The soldiers he was observing were wearing not the standard-issue blue tunics, such as the cavalry he had encountered earlier had been clad in, but rather grey coats and jackets. It looked for all the word as though these men were sporting an altogether new uniform; one which had been designed to set them apart from the usual armed forces of the United States. He was turning this over in his mind and trying to decide what it might mean, when there was a sharp, metallic click a few inches behind his head and a heavily accented voice said softly, 'And now you die, you bastard!'

Harker was lying on his belly, which meant of course that he was also lying on his pistol, which was as usual tucked casually in his belt and was now squashed beneath him. He would not be able to reach it in a hurry and that click he had heard suggested very strongly that the man at his back had already cocked his piece. If only he hadn't been so preoccupied with the camp below, then Harker might have heard this fellow tiptoeing up behind him. He said, 'What say I turn around and face you, so's we can talk like men, face to face.'

'Do that and you're dead,' said the other man. It wasn't proclaimed in an angry or threatening fashion, but in a low, matter-of-fact way that made it all the more chilling. Harker had not the slightest doubt that if he attempted to turn around, he would find a ball flying through the back of his head immediately. The man continued, 'I'm guessing you have a pistol in front, is it not so?'

The 'S's were more like 'Z's, so that 'so' came out as 'zo'. It was this which revealed his antagonist's identity to Harker and he said, 'That would be you, Chappe, am I right?' For answer, he received a crushing blow to the back of his head, delivered with such ferocity that Harker honestly thought for a moment that it might have broken open his skull, allowing his brains to leak out. While he was all but unconscious, the man who had just reversed his carbine and dealt Jed Harker such a savage crack to his head, reached under the dazed man's body and removed the pistol from his belt.

'You best call me *Mr* Chappe,' said Claude Chappe, emphasizing the point by jabbing Harker in the back of his head again. 'Get up. But slowly, slowly if you set any value upon your miserable life.'

There didn't seem anything to do for now, other than follow the little Creole's instructions to the letter. After all, from what Harker could see, the other man held all the cards; at least for this hand. He stood up, feeling giddy and sick from the blow to his head and said, 'You're a brave one, I don't think. Striking a man from behind.'

'Shut up and walk very slowly down into our camp.'

'You want to hand me back my pistol and we'll settle this man to man?'

It was plain that the idea appealed to Chappe, because he did not speak for a few seconds. Then there came a shout from below; the two of them had been spotted. The moment passed and Chappe said, 'Just walk down very, very slowly.'

The arrival of Chappe with his prisoner caused little interest among the men who were erecting the tents and generally preparing the area for some

126

martial activity. Harker cast a practised eye over the field guns and saw that they were six pounders, which he was familiar enough with from the Mexican War. He was surprised; he knew that there was more up-to-date artillery than that about. Why were these people using 1841 model weapons? He did not let it be seen that he had any interest in the disposition of the weaponry here; he'd an idea that that might not be too good for his future health. Instead, he put a bland and slightly dull-witted expression on his face and racked his brains frantically for a good explanation for what he might be doing out here in the wild.

Harker was marched to an officer who, he was intrigued to note, was a full colonel. Not militia either, but regular army by what he could make out. The colonel said to Chappe, 'What's to do? Found a Yankee spy, hey?' His tone of voice was light and suggested to Harker that he did not take his presence there too seriously. Nevertheless, he thought it expedient to make a great show of his protestations.

'Spy?' he exclaimed indignantly, 'I ain't no spy! What in the blazes is going on here?'

'Well now,' said the officer, 'as to that, I reckon it's for you to explain yourself. What was this man about when you took him, Chappe?'

'He was lying on his belly like a snake and watching the camp.'

'Well, sir?' said the colonel, turning to Harker. 'What do you say to that?'

Harker shrugged contemptuously. 'I say it's a lot of

127

hogwash. I had a run-in with this fellow, back in Lovett. Some friends of his stole my horse and so I'm making my way to Kansas on foot. There's no more to the case than that.'

'He's an abolitionist,' said Chappe angrily, 'he took my boy and set him free. Ask him to deny it.'

The colonel held up his hand and said, 'We don't have time for this. Strikes me as you two have some private quarrel. I've bigger fish to fry here. What's your name?'

'Harker. Jed Harker.'

'Well, Mr Harker, I regret to say that I shall have to detain you here for a spell, but no harm will befall you. You must consider yourself a prisoner of war. As soon as we have executed our plans, I promise you'll be freed. You're not the first man to cross swords with Monsieur Chappe here and I doubt you'll be the last. I must have you handcuffed to a wagon or something, until we finish and can eat. Forgive the inconvenience.' He gave an order to the sergeant standing beside him and the man went off, returning a minute later with a pair of bright, steel cuffs.

All considered, things could have been a good deal worse. If he could avoid having his throat cut in the night by the Frenchman, then Harker thought that the colonel seemed like an honourable man, who would be likely to keep his word. He nodded and then went off with Claude Chappe, who was glaring at him venomously. When they reached the nearest cannon, Chappe halted and began trying to force Harker's arms up behind his back, so that he could be secured in the most uncomfortable manner possible. One of the men in grey tunics saw what was going on and came over, saying, 'There's no need for such. If this man's to stay with us for a stretch, we don't need to torture him as well.' He pushed Chappe out of the way and winked at Harker. The soldier secured only one of Harker's wrists to the field gun and said, 'There, you won't be going any-where for a while. Not 'til we've done what's needful, anyway.'

After the man went off, Chappe stood for a space, staring balefully at Harker. It was pretty clear that if the Creole had anything to do with it, then Harker would not be leaving the camp alive.

Once he had been left alone, Harker began think-ing furiously about what might chance, assuming that he was unable to break free of the place. He felt that for his own part, there was a passing fair chance of his making it out of this present fix alive and in one peace. Nobody there, other than Chappe, seemed to be all that ill-disposed towards him and if he could just evade that man's vengeance, then he suspected that he would indeed be freed as soon as these southrons had conducted whatever business it was they had in the area. For after listening to the people here, Harker was sure that every single one of these men came from the south. The colonel's accent was pure Virginia and the rest of them sounded as though they came from Georgia,

Tennessee and so on. Whatever enterprise these men were engaged upon, it was obviously part and parcel of the same set of circumstances which had sent that troop of cavalry racing south.

Taking care of his own self was one thing; Harker was tolerably confident about that. His anxieties centred in the first instance upon Jemima and her children. It would be little short of a tragedy for them if they were snatched back into captivity, just when they were so very nearly free of the toils. Why, it wasn't to be thought of! Then too, there was the matter of Abigail Tyler's revolutionary weapon. If that fell into the hands of these people, then it would most likely be spirited away to some manufactory in the south and reproduced in huge numbers. If the war everybody had been expecting had really begun, then that gun would practically assure the rebels of victory.

Without making a great production of it, Jed Harker began to examine the bonds which held him. The steel shackle would prove impossible to break; he could see that at a glance. It was a standard-issue thing which the army used when restraining an awkward or dangerous prisoner. The thing was designed to hold both wrists, but only Harker's left hand was held. The other shackle was locked to a ring on the field gun. Surreptitiously, he gave a tug on the metal ring, but it was fixed securely. Glancing down casually though, told Harker that the thing was only held onto the wooden spar of the trail by four ordinary screws. He had no screwdriver, but if he could contrive to use something or other, then getting free might not prove all that tricky.

While Harker was turning the matter over in his mind, a grey-coated soldier came up and offered him a mess-tin; filled with an unappetizing and stodgy mound of potatoes and vegetables. Unattractive though the food looked, Harker suddenly realized how hungry he was. The man said, 'Compliments of the colonel.'

'What have I got myself into here?' asked Harker, as he took the proffered food and set it on the ground. It wasn't until you were deprived of the use of one hand, that you found out just how much you depended upon both hands even for so basic and uncomplicated activity as eating.

'We's aheadin' north,' said the man in a friendly enough way. 'Fighting's begun down in Charleston and so we's making sure as this border's secure.'

This boy couldn't have been above nineteen years of age and from the way he spoke, Harker guessed that he was just a farmer's son. He said, 'Mind if I ask your regiment?' Seeing the guarded and suspicious look which came into the fellow's eyes when he asked this question, he hastily followed it by saying, 'I ask because I used to belong to a regiment down south, some years back. The Third Kentucky Horse.'

The boy's eyes lit up at this information and he exclaimed happily, 'Why, you don't say so. My pa, he was in the Kentucky Horse. Happen you knew him? Name of Carter, Nathanial Carter.'

'I don't recollect the name, but then he was most like a little before my time. I was in the Mexican War.'

'You ain't a southerner though, are you?'

'No, it's by way of being a long story. So you folk are heading north? You going right up to Kansas?'

The young man scratched his head and said slowly, 'Well, they don't tell us all that they plan, but yeah, I reckon that's about the strength of it.'

The afternoon dragged on, with nobody taking any particular notice of the prisoner secured to the field gun. There was drilling, latrines were dug, fires built and the usual activity which one would expect to see in a temporary camp of this sort. Harker watched what was going on with the practised eye of a former soldier. The piece of ordnance to which he was shackled had been set up about fifty yards from the tents and so he was a little out of the way and could not hear much of what was said by the men in the encampment. A couple of times, Claude Chappe wandered up and, without saying a word, drew his finger across his throat as though cutting it. By which, Jed Harker understood pretty well that as soon as he had the opportunity, the Creole meant to murder him.

At dusk, some more food and water were brought to the prisoner and after that, he was seemingly forgotten about. It was a chilly night and the soldiers were huddled around camp fires. A crescent moon, combined with a cloudy and overcast sky meant that the darkness was complete. Harker listened carefully, for he fully expected Chappe to sneak up and slit his throat in the dark and he was not intending to be taken unawares. So it was that when he heard stealthy sounds, suggestive of somebody creeping slowly towards him, he turned to face the danger and resolved that if it was the Frenchman, then he would sell his life dearly. It was an enormous shock, although also a great relief, when he heard Pompey's husky voice whispering, 'You awake, Jed?'

'Lord almighty boy,' he replied softly, 'What in the hell are you doing here? I'd hoped that you and your ma would o' set a good way from this place by now.'

'We wouldn't leave you here, sir,' said the boy reproachfully, 'neither me nor ma would hear on it.'

Jed Harker's brain had begun to work furiously, as soon as he realized that he had an ally near at hand. He said, 'it's surely a forlorn hope, but you wouldn't happen to have such an article as a screwdriver on you, I suppose?'

'Got my pocket-knife. That have a blade with a flat head.'

'Could I have it, d'you think?'

'Sure can.' Pompey reached into his pocket and then crawled closer to the gun and handed it over to Harker. It was too dark for either of them to see anything other than the faintest silhouette, but Jed Harker smiled warmly. He located the screws by feeling with his fingertips and then proceeded to undo them, freeing the metal ring, to which he was attached, from the trail of the field-gun. Having done this, Harker closed the flat-headed blade and, again working by touch alone, opened the largest blade; which he tested with his finger. It was, as far as he could tell, razor-sharp.

It was a relief to be able to stand up freely, even if the chunk of metal around his left wrist was something of an encumbrance. Taking Pompey's arm, he guided the boy in the direction that he thought they should be moving; which was to say, away from the camp. The less talking they did, the better. There had been no warning shouts from any of the men seated around the various campfires which twinkled in the shallow valley between the hills. It was Harker's feeling that they had forgotten all about him and most likely would not be overly distressed were he to make off.

One person though had not forgotten about Jed Harker, for as he and Pompey made their way up the gentle slope leading to the crown of trees at the top, a dark shadow reared up, from where it had been lying and most likely observing them. At that moment, the clouds parted and the feeble light of the moon shone through. Harker and the boy found themselves face to face with Claude Chappe, who had in his hand a pistol.

CHAPTER 8

The Creole did not even bother to point his pistol at them. The boy, who knew how cruel his former master was, drew closer to Harker, seeking protection. Chappe said, 'Yes, I thought it worth waiting here. I'd an idea I'd catch more than one bird that way.'

Had it been only his own life at stake, Harker might have hesitated a little before taking the action he did. But he was only too well aware that if this devil remained alive and free, then this helpless boy would once again become, leastways according to the law, his 'property'. It was not to be borne. There was little point in parlaying and having made his decision, Jed Harker saw no cause for further delay. He sprang forward and then swept the knife he was gripping in a wide arc; slashing through Claude Chappe's throat with no more difficulty than if he had been cutting wheat with a sickle. Then he dropped the knife and shot out his hand to grab the pistol and pluck it from the dying man's unresisting fingers. As Chappe fell to his hands and knees, gurgling and spraying blood from the severed artery in his neck, Harker remarked in a helpful tone of voice, 'Talking's one thing. Fighting's something else again. Doesn't do to mix 'em up.'

Pompey stood transfixed. For all that he had conceived a great liking and admiration for Harker, the swiftness and savagery of the attack had taken him aback and he started in horror at the scene. Chappe did not even have the strength now to remain on his hands and knees and had collapsed, face down, in a heap.

Picking up the boy's pocket-knife, Harker closed the blade back into the handle and handed it to Pompey, saying, 'That's an ugly thing to see, but it'd be a sight uglier, were you to be at that man's mercy again.' This was undeniably true and so the boy dropped the knife back in his pocket and set off up the hill with Harker. Once they were over the crest and heading down the other side, it seemed safe to speak in low tones and Pompey told him what had chanced since he was captured.

It appeared that the boy had followed Harker on his abortive hunting expedition, trailing behind him at a fair distance. The chance of watching his hero in action with a firearm had lured him on in this way. So it was that he had seen Chappe take Harker prisoner and when the two men had disappeared from sight over the hill, Pompey had crept up and spied out the camp, seeing where his friend had been fixed to the cannon. Harker was overcome with genuine amazement and gratitude. He said, 'You took the hell of a risk, son. You might o' be seen and dragged back into captivity yourself.'

'You risk your life for me. I didn't do no more than you done for me.'

Although not given to emotion, Jed Harker felt a lump in his throat on hearing this. It was uncommon enough for anybody, let alone a child, to speak so to him. He swallowed hastily and said in a gruff tone, 'Well, it won't be forgot. You're a damned good comrade, Pompey and that's the least I can say. You saved my life, for that man would have killed me, had I been left there helpless. Where are the rest of the folks now?'

Apparently, the wagon was waiting about a mile away. Although he didn't say so outright, it was Harker's impression that Abigail Tyler had been all for riding on to Kansas and leaving him to his fate. This did not really surprise him; she had made it clear that she was not overly keen on him. However, both Jemima and her son had remained firm that under no circumstances would they agree to such a course of action. Since Abigail could not really abandon the family in the middle of the territories, she had been obliged to wait until nightfall, when Pompey had set off to see what he could do about freeing Harker.

Because it was so dark, it was impossible to see the

expressions on Abigail Tyler and Jemima's faces when Jed Harker and Pompey fetched up, back at the wagon. Jemima murmured piously, 'Thank the Lord.'

For her part, Abigail contented herself with saying ungraciously, 'Well, now you're back, I guess we can make a start. Though Lord knows I've no appetite for travelling in the dark. From what young Pompey tells me though, there's a heap o' southerners near at hand, with artillery and I don't know what-all else.'

'That's about the strength of it,' admitted Harker, 'and I think that your plan of moving a bit by night is a sound one. I surely hope we don't bust an axle doing it though.'

It turned out that Harker was the only one who had had any hot food since earlier that day, when they had eaten at Abbot's place. The baby was all right, he was still not weaned, but the two women and the boy had only shared the one loaf of bread since then. There was little to be done about it, for he couldn't hunt at night. Nor, he supposed, would it be wise to do so even when the sun had risen the next day. In the state of heightened tension which evidently obtained throughout that part of the Indian Nations, any sound of shooting stood a good chance of attracting unwelcome attention.

They steered a course north, by the fitful glimpses of the moon which were seen from time to time when the clouds parted. After a couple of hours, Harker said, 'I reckon we might be best advised to stop now and make a right early start in the morning, no later than sun-up.' It was a hungry and fearful little group who settled down to snatch what sleep they were able; given the unpromising circumstances.

The next day, Harker was awake before dawn. The sky was a clear, dark blue which gave him reason to hope that it was going to be a fine, sunny day, ideally suited for travelling. He roused the others briskly, eager to be off at once. If the two oxen could only be persuaded to bestir themselves, he didn't despair of the possibility that they might cross into Kansas that very night.

It was a miserable beginning to the journey, not having any food at all with which to break their fast. Still, there was nothing to be done about it. They would have to hope that something turned up later; although who or what might provide them with sustenance in the middle of the territories was more than Jed Harker was prepared to adventure a guess on. As it was, their bellies were hungry now and so they might as well be hungry while travelling as being hungry there and just sitting and bemoaning their ill fortune.

'Pompey, you and me can walk, while the ladies ride in the wagon,' said Harker. 'Times such as this, we have to look to the weakest of the party and aid them how we are able.'

Hungry and tired as he was, the boy glowed with happiness at Harker's words, for it was obvious that he was being treated as a man; one who had to make sacrifices so that the women of the party could be looked after.

They were on the move before the sun rose and it was not a pleasant or enjoyable journey for anybody. There was plenty of water, but nothing else; not so much as a morsel of food. Harker had gone on short commons often enough in his life that the prospect did not worry him unduly now. He kept an anxious eye on Pompey, who strode along manfully at his side, but the boy looked as though he too were going to be fit for a march on an empty stomach. When a sudden improvement in their prospects came, it was out of the blue and wholly without warning.

Being slightly elevated on the seat of the wagon gave Abigail Tyler a better view of the land ahead than Harker. He, in any case, was trudging along just then without really paying any heed to the horizon. He was engaged in a conversation with young Pompey, the aim of which was to take the boy's mind off his hunger. The first that Harker knew was that Abigail said sharply, 'There's some wagon or cart ahead.' The same thought struck them all; suppose this was more soldiers from the south?

Harker said, 'Well, we're off the road, so happen this is another soul who don't want to get caught up with any trouble. Rein in, Miss Tyler.' He went over to the back of the wagon and took out the carbine, checking that it was loaded. Then he said, 'You two women best get down and shelter behind the wagon, least 'til we see what's what. Pompey, can you use a pistol?'

'Sho' can!'

'Then take this, which was your boss's and we'll see what chances. Don't fire a shot though, unless I start, is that plain?' He handed the boy Chappe's gun.

Pompey nodded, overjoyed to be standing next to his hero, with a gun in his hand and being treated like a grown-up person.

It was a horse and cart coming along the valley floor towards them and when it was a mile or so away, Harker laughed and said, 'Well, these'll give us no trouble. They're missioners, by the look of them.' As the cart drew a little closer, the others could see that he was right and that two men, both clad soberly in clerical black, were sitting at the front of the cart. They continued towards Harker and his group, taking a quarter hour or so to reach them. As they came nearer, it could be seen that both men in the cart were priests. They reined in their horse when they were twenty yards or so off from the people whose wagon was right across their path. One of the men called out cheerfully, a broad smile on his face, 'What's to do? Is it an ambush?'

Jed Harker walked over to the men, holding the musket casually under his arm, but ready to raise it and fire, should these newcomers prove to be travelling under a false flag. He had heard of men dressing as missionaries or priests to deceive the unwary, who were then robbed or even murdered. These two had honest, open faces, but there was no percentage in taking any chances. He said, 'We're heading into

141

Kansas. You might want to know that there's an army camp ahead.'

'Federal or southrons?'

'Southerners. They're up to some game or other in blocking the border north of here.'

While they were speaking, Harker could not help but notice that the cart which the priests were driving looked to be loaded with provisions. There were round loaves of flat-bread, wheels of cheese and haunches of meat. He said, 'You men opening a store or something?'

One of the priests laughed and said, 'It's been a bare winter. Some of our parishioners are nigh to starving. We're taking stuff to a village near here.'

Although it went very much against the grain for Jed Harker to ask a favour of any man, he had to think not only of himself, but the women and children. He said, 'I sure hate to ask, but there's two hungry women and a boy back by the wagon. They've not ate for a while and at this rate, they'll be going hungry 'til we reach the border. I don't suppose you could spare just a little for them?'

'Black family, hey?' said one of the men. 'You working for the underground railroad?'

'Not exactly,' replied Harker ruefully, 'it's by way of being a long story.'

'Well, you and us are in the same game,' said the other priest. 'We can surely provide you with enough to reach Kansas. Call your friends over and they can take enough for a day or two.'

It was exceedingly pleasant to encounter folks that wished to aid, rather than hinder him and although he didn't in general like taking help from strangers, Jed Harker had a warm feeling from the transaction. After the men had given them enough bread and cheese, along with a hunk of salted meat, to satisfy them for the next few days, Harker said, 'I can't thank you fellows enough. I owe you.'

One of the priests laughed at that, saying, 'You don't owe us a thing. We're all labouring in the Lord's vineyard, doing his work.' They parted amiably.

While Harker and the others made a late breakfast (they were all ravenously hungry), he outlined what had been said and remarked to Abigail Tyler, 'That's the first time I been accused of doing the Lord's work! That's a rare novelty.'

To Harker's immense surprise, Jemima spoke and said, 'You doin' the Lord's work, all right. Don' it say in scripture about folk entertainin' angels unawares? I reckon that you're a one of 'em.'

This was so unexpected, the woman not having spoken more than a couple of words at a time before this, that for a moment Harker was at a loss to know how to respond. At length, he said, 'Well, ma'am, it's right kind of you to give me such a character, but I reckon I never yet been mistook for an angel!'

Pompey said in a low voice, 'My ma's right. You been sent from on high to guard us.'

This was frankly embarrassing and Harker

143

changed the subject, saying briskly, 'Well, if you've all ate your fill, I think as we should get moving. The more distance between us and that camp o' soldiers, the better I'll like it.'

The day progressed somewhat more cheerfully, now that they all had full bellies. Harker took a turn at driving the oxen; whipping them mercilessly to try and speed up the pace a little. At the back of his mind he was uneasily aware that he had committed murder not twelve hours since and if any of Claude Chappe's friends were very fond of him, they might be inclined to avenge his death. It was a little after noon that another group of travellers appeared ahead of them. By this time, Jed Harker had figured that moving quickly was more important than travelling in secret. He had accordingly begun steering a little to the west, so that they were now leaving the hills and moving back towards the track that led towards Kansas. The track was just a little ahead of them to their left and in the distance they could see what looked like a line of wagons or carts heading in their way. Harker felt uneasy. He halted the wagon and said, 'Well, it's too late to scuttle back into those hills to hide. We'll just have to hope that these are friends.

There were a half dozen wagons and as they came closer, the dark blue of army uniforms could be made out. This looked promising and unless he was very much mistaken, Harker thought that these men meant no harm to either him or those for whom he

144

was caring. He urged the oxen on until they joined the track. Then he waited for the troops to reach them.

There were five wagons and it turned out that they were part of a Commissary Department detail, carrying food and other supplies to the forces which had already entered the Indian Nations and were now operating in the south of the territory. One was a chuck-wagon and the others contained provisions. So, at any rate, the lead driver told him when the carts drew level with Harker's own wagon. There were only ten men in the whole outfit; five to drive and a man riding shotgun on each. It struck Harker that this was a terrible arrangement and that these men would be vulnerable to any attack. The men driving were not even real soldiers, being no more than cooks, who were seldom expected to do anything warlike. Even the 'guards' were young men; so young that they did not even appear to be shaving yet. Whoever had organized this expedition must have been relying upon an awful lot of good fortune, if he thought that these carts had a better than fifty-fifty chance of getting to their destination unmolested. A minute later and it was tolerably plain to Harker that the odds were even worse than that, for a group of grey-clad riders appeared on the crest of one of the hills that he and his friends had lately left. This did not bode well.

The man he was chatting to did not look to Harker as though he fully grasped the significance of the

145

riders up on the ridge above them. Harker said, 'You boys might want to prepare for some lively action. Those fellows are the ones you're supposed to be putting a halt to.' He scanned the hills again, hoping that the southerners wouldn't have hauled their field-guns up there and be using them to cover the road north. There was no sign of such a move, although more riders looked to be joining the group which he had first noticed. Those were the men in whose camp he had briefly been detained, if he was any judge of it. He wondered vaguely if they had been pursuing him, because of the death of the little Frenchman. But there, they most likely had bigger fish than him to fry. They had probably been ordered to choke off supplies passing south along this track. He turned to Abigail Tyler, who was seated at his side and said, 'We best break out those guns o' your'n again, Miss Tyler. I'd be mighty surprised if those boys aren't about to ride down on us.'

The men on the other wagons were taking notice now and cocking their pieces, in case there was going to be shooting. As for Harker, he reached back into the wagon and took out one of Abigail's weapons. The soldier to whom he had been speaking said, 'Jesus Christ, what's that you got there?'

Harker didn't bother to answer, but took out the other gun and said to Abigail Tyler, 'You were all-fired keen on what you was pleased to call "a field test" not so long since. You'd best get ready for another.'

'I can't fire this,' she exclaimed, aghast, 'not after what I saw before!'

Harker stared hard at her and said, 'You're fixin' for to see the United States army having these things. You're afraid to use it yourself?'

Reluctantly, she took it from his hands and the two of them climbed down from the buckboard and took up positions behind the wagon. Harker said to Jemima and Pompey, 'You two had best get behind the carts here, in case there's lead flying about. You'll be safer there.'

Pompey was disposed to argue the point, feeling shamed to be sent off with his mother and baby brother. He said, 'I can help. I can fire this here pistol.'

'Pistols is all right for close quarter work, son, but next to useless at the range we're going to be engaging at. I'd feel easier in my mind knowing that you're guarding your ma and keeping her safe.'

Something about Harker's tone of voice told the boy that this was one of those times for taking orders and doing as he was bid. He said, 'Come on, Ma, I'll protect you.' The family went round to the back of the wagons, leaving Harker free to concentrate on the peril which faced them.

Reluctant as he was to take command, Harker feared that if nobody was decisive, then the encounter with the southern riders was apt to be a shambles. Since he had a stake in the affair, he supposed that it fell to him to arrange matters. He said to the young soldiers and men who had been driving the carts, 'You'd best all get behind your wagons and prepare to drive off those men, should they take it into their heads to ride down on us.' The men seemed relieved to find that there was somebody who would give orders. As they followed his advice and began moving to cover, Harker said sharply, 'And listen to what I tell you. Me and this lady are going to be staying here, just a little in front of some of you. Mind what you're about, if it comes to shooting. I've no mind to be caught between two enemies. Mind you don't hit us.'

No sooner were these words out of Jed Harker's mouth, than the men up on the ridge began moving down towards them. By Harker's estimate, there were some forty riders. He guessed that most were regular army who had thrown in their lot with the south. Well, this was where the knife met the bone. He cocked the strange gun and sighted down the barrel.

CHAPTER 9

The troop of riders seemed to be in no particular hurry. The hill was not a steep one and they just trotted down at a steady and relaxed pace. There was a deadly and determined air about these men. They were competent and assured and perhaps felt more than able to tackle a handful of men from the Commissary Department. For one thing, they out-numbered them four or five to one, for another they were regular soldiers used to fighting. The boys facing them were volunteers who had not been long in uniform. Harker gauged this by the bristling beards and bushy moustaches sported by many of those heading towards them. These were not green boys.

'Think you'll be able to fire, when the time comes?' Harker said quietly to Abigail Tyler.

'It's my skin at stake, well as yours,' she replied shortly. 'Those boys make off with these guns and my plans and it'll mean ruination for the United States.'

There was no time for any further conversation because the cavalry had halted about a hundred yards away. They were not strung out in a line, but were all gathered together in a compact body. One of the riders walked his horse forward alone, shouting in a loud, clear voice, 'It's a parlay! Don't fire.' When he was twenty yards from the line of wagons, this man said in a commanding tone, 'It'll be all up with you fellows if we should attack you. We have field-guns up in the hills yonder, as could finish the job, even if we fall. It needn't come to shooting though.'

Since there didn't appear to be anybody else on their side who was planning to respond to this, Harker thought that the duty probably devolved upon him and so he called back, 'What will you have? There's only food in these wagons, supplies and such.'

'Don't fox with me,' said the southerner. 'We want those guns that I see you and your friend have. We get them and the plans for them and Miss Tyler along of them, we'll engage to leave the rest of you in peace.'

'You think we'd yield up a lady under the threat of force?' asked Harker in amazement. 'We'd sooner die fighting around her. I never heard such a thing.'

'I swear she'll come to no harm. We'll treat her honourable. We can't have her going off though and teaching others how to make those guns.'

Harker called sternly, 'I never heard the like. You think any of us men would agree to surrender a lady

150

in that way? Be off with you!'

The southron's face was a picture of baffled fury. At length, without saying another word, he wheeled his horse around and trotted back to his companions. Harker said softly, 'You ready for action? If it comes, then you sweep in from your side and I'll do the same from mine.' Abigail nodded. Harker called back to the men behind him, 'You boys ready, if they want to make a fight of it?' There were various grunts, which he took to indicate agreement. Harker couldn't help but get the impression though that there was a lack of enthusiasm for the whole business. Perhaps those youngsters thought that they had been drawn into a private dispute, about which they knew nothing. In a sense, of course, they were perfectly correct.

Once the man to whom they had been speaking rejoined the other riders, there was a pause, as he had a brief conversation with his friends. Then, a bugle sounded and the horsemen divided into two groups and began trotting forward; clearly meaning to outflank them and sweep in from the rear. At another note from the bugle, the trot became a canter and time had run out to do anything other than start fighting. Peering down the barrel of his weapon, which was resting conveniently on the side of the wagon, Harker took aim at the man on his far right and squeezed the trigger.

It was the ferocious and ear-splitting noise which really took Harker aback, despite having already used the gun before. The rapid hammering truly sounded like an iron foundry going at full pelt. As soon as Harker fired, Abigail Tyler opened up as well. So tremendous was the roar of those two weapons, that it was quite impossible to know if the soldiers behind them were also firing their carbines. One immediate effect of the firing was that Harker was aware of sudden, frantic movement to one side. The oxen were placid creatures; not easily stirred to unnecessary movement. Indeed, it was hard enough to get them to move at any time. Not so the horses which were harnessed up to the chuck-wagon and other carts. The sudden, almighty din caused them to panic and bolt. From the very edge of his field of vision, Harker caught a glimpse of frenzied activity, as the five wagons belonging to the army began lurching away. There was little to be done about that though, for all Harker's attention was focused now upon doing as much harm as could be to his adversaries.

The momentum of the riders carried them forward, despite the death of some of the riders. Jed Harker knew that the most effective way of halting the charge would be to aim at the horses, rather than the riders, but he could not bring himself to do so. They were, after all, just innocent, dumb beasts. Although he and Abigail had accounted for a number of the men charging at them, there were simply too many to expect that they could all be taken out. Some had managed to outflank them and ride around the side, where Harker could only hope that the soldiers behind him might take care of them. One riderless horse crashed into the wagon behind which Harker and Abigail were sheltering. Then another careered past, with a wounded man being dragged along screaming, bouncing along the ground with his foot caught in the stirrup.

Having used up all the ammunition in Abigail's gun, Harker tossed it down and snatched up the rifle which he had used a few days ago. Even though he could hear the crackle of musketry behind him, after the racket those guns made, it was blessedly quiet. There were no riders active before him and so Harker turned to see what was going on elsewhere. He was in time to see a dozen or so of the opposing force cantering off out of range. The soldiers who had been accompanying the wagons had evidently been firing to some good effect.

Since there was no more fighting to be done, Jed Harker thought that it was time to reckon up the damage. Jemima and her boys were safe and well. Having established this, Harker went back to see how Abigail Tyler had fared. She too was all right, if a little pale and shaken. She was such a tough nut in the usual way of things, that Harker could not resist saying, 'I guess that was lively enough for you?' She shot him a venomous look and he went off to inspect the field of battle. It didn't take long for him to total up the casualties; twenty-nine horses and thirty-one men.

One thing which Jed Harker thought most remarkable was that only three of these men were wounded; the rest of them lay stone dead. This was a far greater kill-rate than one would ever see with more conventional weaponry. He attributed it to the exploding bullets which Abigail Tyler had devised. Presumably, when they burst open, they ruptured any nearby blood vessels. With such things, there would be no flesh wounds. Being struck anyway on the trunk or the upper parts of the limbs would be sure to result in death from loss of blood.

Of those who had been injured, one had merely fallen off his horse and was badly bruised. The other two had minor puncture wounds in their calves. Provided the wounds were dressed and no infection developed, they would probably be all right. While he was examining the corpses and offering reassurance to those who had survived, one of the soldiers from the supply wagons came over to talk to Harker. It was clear that he was not happy. He said, 'You let us play some part in a game o' your own. T'weren't us those men were after, it was you and your friends.'

'Never said otherwise,' replied Harker, guiltily aware that he hadn't been entirely straight with these people. 'You assumed what you did, I never said nothing.'

'One o' my friends back there, he's broke his leg. Horse bolted and took the wagon over m'friend's leg. Snapped it clean in half.'

'I'm sorry to hear it, I hope that he'll heal up fine.

By the by, what about these men? They're injured.'

'You shot 'em. You can tend to 'em.'

There was no sign of the attackers who had galloped off in such haste. It seemed to Harker likely that they had circled round and gone back to the hills. Would they make good on the threat of bringing their artillery into play? Jed Harker thought it would be foolish to linger in the vicinity to find out. He left the injured men and went over to Abigail, saying, 'I think we should dig up, right now.'

'I think you're right,' she said. 'Will you get Jemima and her boys?'

Pompey was excited at the gun battle, being of an age to find such things a thrilling novelty. It turned out that he had actually fired the pistol on his own account, at a rider who he felt was coming to close to him and his ma. He hadn't hit the man, but never-the-less felt that this made him an active participant in the affair. Harker listened patiently and let the boy run on for a spell, before saying sincerely, 'You did well, son. Better than well. You've the makings of a fine man. We best be making tracks, before anybody fetches reinforcements.'

The mood of the soldiers in charge of the supply wagons was not favourable to either Jed Harker or his friends. The young man who'd been run over by the runaway wagon was in considerable pain and this too did not endear Harker to anybody. They all felt, with some justification, that it was he who had called the lightning down upon them. When he and his wagon left, there were no fond farewells.

Although he had toyed with the notion of taking the wounded southerners along with him, in the end Harker left them to the military to deal with. He was relieved when a couple of miles down the road, they encountered a squad of blue-coated cavalry, to whom he gave a simplified version of the events which had lately befallen their comrades in arms. It looked to Harker as though this area at least was now firmly under control of the United States regular forces and that they would not be molested before reaching Kansas. An hour after they parted from the cavalry, they came to a wide river, which wound its way along their left. Harker reined in the oxen and said to Abigail Tyler, who was seated at his side, 'You and me need to talk.'

Jemima and Pompey watched silently as Harker led the woman to the edge of the river. When they were out of earshot of the others, Harker said, 'Those weapons of yours have caused me to kill more men in a few days than I did throughout the whole course of the Mexican war. Give those to the government in Washington and two things'll happen.'

After her own part in the death of over thirty men, Abigail Tyler was more subdued than she had been since Harker had first picked up with her. She said, 'What's that?'

'First off is where Mr Lincoln will be unbeatable, when once he starts a manufactory for your guns. He'll sweep through the south, but he won't stop there. He'll most like want a bit of Mexico too. Then, when he falls out with the English, it'll be a slice of Canada. I don't know a heap about politics, but I know how such things work.'

'What else?' asked Abigail in a low, dispirited tone.

'Others'll get them too. Thing like that, spies will take it. You'll end up with two sets of men facing each other, both armed with your guns. The killing will be worse than you can imagine.'

For the space of a minute or so, Abigail Tyler did not speak, but then she said, 'You think I'm a fool. Not to have seen all that for my own self.'

'Nothing of the sort. You're not a soldier, you don't know how these things work, is all. But you've seen enough deaths in the last few days to show you where the wind will blow, if once your invention is common knowledge.'

'What would you have me do?'

Jed Harker said, 'You want my advice? We break up those things and pitch them in the river. Then we burn the plans.'

Abigail thought this proposition over for a bit and then said, 'You're right, of course. I was dreaming of saving the world and being famous and I don't know what all else. All I've done is end up killing a heap of folk. Let's do it.'

Together, Harker and Abigail fetched the two guns from the wagon and then, using the tools from the chest beneath the wagon-seat, they took them to pieces, throwing each part as far out into the river as could be. Then Abigail fetched the plans which she had so painstakingly drawn up and Harker struck a Lucifer. Together, they watched them burn to ashes. Then they went back to the wagon and Harker suggested that Jemima and Pompey might want a turn riding.

As they strolled north along the track to Kansas, Harker said to Abigail Tyler, 'I'll warrant you've other ideas in that head of yours, maybe less likely to end up killing folk.'

'Oh, any number,' she said with false gaiety, obviously still a little sad about the end of her grand schemes for making the world a better and safer place. 'I've one in especial, a device for using type without a printing press. So that people can print in their own homes or offices. I even drew up some sketches a while back.'

'I've an idea that might be a better scheme than weaponry,' remarked Harker laconically. 'Less apt to kill folks, I mean.'

As he chatted in a desultory way with the woman at his side, Harker glanced over to the wagon, where Pompey and his ma were riding. He could see that they were mightily interested in what he and Abigail Tyler could be saying. Perhaps they thought that he would throw in his hand with Abigail and abandon them as soon as they reached Kansas; but he wasn't such a dog as that. It was his intention to stick with that family every step of the way, until he was certain-sure that they were safely settled out of harm's way in the north. And then what?

Jed Harker looked across the plain to the distant horizon. He had been heading this way before coming across Abigail Tyler and her strange invention. Once he'd seen Jemima and her children safe in somebody else's care, he would be able to continue his wanderings and once again be a free agent, responsible for nobody but his own self and beholden to nobody on God's earth. It was a heartrending and alluring prospect.